My Best Friend's Stepfather

Books by Opal Carew

My Best Friend's Stepfather

Opal Carew

ST. MARTIN'S GRIFFIN

NEW YORK

MY BEST FRIEND'S STEPFATHER. Copyright © 2015 by Opal Carew. All rights reserved. Printed in the United States of America. For information, address St. Martin's Press, 175 Fifth Avenue, New York, N.Y. 10010.

www.stmartins.com

Library of Congress Cataloging-in-Publication Data

Names: Carew, Opal.
Title: My best friend's stepfather / Opal Carew.
Description: First edition. | New York : St. Martin's Griffin, 2016.
Identifiers: LCCN 2015037620| ISBN 9781250052865 (trade paperback) | ISBN 9781466854727 (e-book)
Subjects: LCSH: Sexual dominance and submission—Fiction. | Triangles (Interpersonal relations)—Fiction. | Man-woman relationships—Fiction. | BISAC: FICTION / Romance / Adult. | FICTION / Romance / Contemporary. | GSAFD: Erotic fiction.
Classification: LCC PR9199.4.C367 M9 2016 | DDC 813/.6—dc23
LC record available at http://lccn.loc.gov/2015037620

Our books may be purchased in bulk for promotional, educational, or business use. Please contact your local bookseller or the Macmillan Corporate and Premium Sales Department at (800) 221-7945, extension 5442, or by e-mail at MacmillanSpecialMarkets@macmillan.com.

First Edition: January 2016

10 9 8 7 6 5 4 3 2 1

*In loving memory of my sister Dale,
who brightened my childhood with
the light of a thousand suns.*

Acknowledgments

As always, my heartfelt thanks to Rose Hilliard and Emily Sylvan Kim for your support and inspiration. And to Mark, Matt, and Jason, thank you for your love and support. I'd also like to thank my family, who is always there when I need them.

Part One

"Did you just say you want to be a Domme?" Adam asked in disbelief. His feet hit the ground at a steady pace as they ran along the paved path in the park.

Of course he knew that couldn't possibly be what Ashley had said. Not Ash.

"I didn't say I want to be a Domme," Ash said, her breathing a bit labored.

He slowed down and she kept pace beside him. Usually she could easily do this pace, but she seemed a little off today. Nervous.

"I said that I'm going to meet with a Dom."

Adam's chest tightened. Why would Ashley want to see a Dom? Was she going to get into some kinky sexual thing? His heart thumped louder than the running accounted for.

"The man is only in town for a couple of months on business. Apparently he's active in the BDSM lifestyle. I heard about him through a friend," she went on to say. "She said he's a little intense, but I'll be in good hands."

Adam held back a scowl. He didn't want her in anyone's

hands but his own. Fuck, he should pull her into a swel-tering kiss right now, then show her exactly what it would be like to be dominated—by him.

He'd been attracted to Ash for a long time, but he'd met her when she was sixteen and he was in his twenties, and she was his friend's younger sister, so he'd never pur-sued a relationship with her. When she'd returned from college looking for a job, he'd hired her at the magazine and they'd become friends. But the fact that he was her boss had kept him from asking her out.

But that didn't stop him from getting jealous when she was with someone else.

And protective. Her seeing someone who would dom-inate her didn't sit well with him.

"Why are you telling me this?"

"You told me I could do a special-interest piece for the magazine and I've been looking for something different. I thought I'd talk about the popularity of BDSM in romance novels. Discuss what really happens in this type of rela-tionship. And I thought it would be a fun angle to . . . you know, talk to a real-life Christian Grey about the whole lifestyle. This man is a wealthy guy, owns a huge corpo-ration, and he's into domination. I think our readers would love it."

His chest constricted. The guy reminded him of some-one from his past. Someone he did not want to think about. He frowned.

Ashley glanced at her friend Adam. She had bungled this conversation.

Maybe she'd become too relaxed about their friendship versus their work relationship. Would he be more amenable to the idea if she'd pitched it in the office, not running through the park? Or did he really not like the idea?

She really did think it was a great idea that their readers would enjoy. And she was excited about researching it. Her heart pounded at the thought of seeing Darien Gallagher and talking about kinky sexual stuff. It would be strange and awkward, but at the same time exciting.

She hoped she could convince Adam to let her go forward with it.

She gazed at Adam's profile. His perfect, straight nose, the curve of his full lips, his strong chin. A lock of his chestnut brown hair had fallen on his forehead, as it often did, and he pushed it back. A familiar ache filled her. She'd had a longtime crush on him. Ever since she was a teenager. He was her brother Brad's hot friend. Of course, he'd paid no attention to her back then. He'd been friendly and polite—and sometimes she would imagine she'd see a spark in his eyes when he glanced her way—but she'd convinced herself that it was just her imagination. Seeing what she wanted to see.

Now, years later, since they'd started working together, they'd become close friends. But that hadn't stopped the attraction she felt for him from growing.

He slowed his pace, then headed toward an empty bench facing the river. She followed him. He must have noticed her breathing was a little heavy. He always watched out for her like that. That was one of the things she loved about him.

Adam sat down and she sat beside him.

"Don't you like the idea?"

"Of you going to see some guy who might handcuff you and get rough with you?"

"Just to make it clear. It's not a sexual thing," she explained. "It's just research for an article. Look, I know you worry about me, but I can handle myself and I know he's safe."

His piercing brown eyes locked on hers. "How do you know that?"

"I told you. My friend knows him very well."

"Is this friend Jessica?" he asked.

She raised a brow. "Don't you trust Jessica's judgment?"

Her question was an evasive maneuver. Jessica didn't know Mr. Gallagher very well at all, but she wasn't going to say too much. Adam had worked for Darien Gallagher on an internship one summer when he was in college and whenever she'd asked him about it afterward, he'd closed up. He avoided talking about the internship or Mr. Gallagher, a mystery that one day she'd like to solve.

But for now, she would not mention his name because she didn't want Adam to turn down this project.

Adam leaned back on the bench. "I know Jessica looks out for you."

He stared at the trees across the path from them, clearly thinking. He didn't seem happy and, other than his protectiveness of her, she wasn't sure why. He was usually right on board to try something edgy.

She gazed at him with wide eyes. "You said you'd give me a chance to do something new. To broaden my horizons. Please, Adam. Let me do this."

         •   •   •

Ashley pulled into the driveway of the stately, gray brick house. An immaculate garden lined the curved walkway leading from the interlock brick driveway to the entrance.

She pulled down the visor and glanced in the mirror. Her dark auburn hair was a bit mussed, so she grabbed the brush from her purse and ran it through the long waves that flowed past her shoulders. She reapplied her burgundy lipstick, too. Then she opened the car door and got out.

As she followed the walkway her stomach fluttered. She shifted her purse to her other hand. She was more than a little nervous about this meeting with Darien Gallagher. What she hadn't told Adam was that the friend that knew Mr. Gallagher very well was her and Jessica's best friend, Helen. Because he was her stepfather.

At least, he used to be. When she and Jessica and Helen were in high school, Helen's mother had remarried. The man, who was quite a bit younger than Helen's mother, was rich, mysterious, and intensely sexy. He had this air of authority that sent quivers along her spine, and his aloofness made her long to uncover his secrets.

When he and Helen's mother had come to their graduation, every girl in school had drooled over him. His devastating good looks and air of authority had made Ash's heart somersault every time she'd seen him. Even though he was older, Ash had had inappropriate fantasies about the man.

The thought of him made her even more nervous now.

She walked up the three steps to the front door. The entrance was stunning, with a stained-glass door and matching sidelights in a simple diamond pattern.

When she used to go over to Helen's to hang out, she'd always been conscious of his presence. He was usually working in his den, but sometimes she'd see him when he went to get a drink, or he'd be reading the paper in the living room. Sometimes when Helen's mom would invite her over for dinner, she'd feel his gaze on her, sending quivers down her spine.

Once she caught sight of him taking a swim in the pool and she'd been astonished at his hard, muscular body. To her shock, she'd had hot dreams of him that night.

She'd always felt self-conscious around him. He was Jessica's stepfather. Tall, gorgeous, and intimidating. Not that he'd ever tried to intimidate her. Her heart thumped as she remembered how he would look at her with those dark, unreadable midnight blue eyes and smile. In those instants, she'd always felt like the most special person in the world.

She knew it had just been her fantasizing. She was just a friend of his stepdaughter's. He was polite, but she was barely of notice to him.

Now he'd agreed to help her with her article and she was thankful for that.

She sighed and knocked on the door.

The door opened and Ashley found herself gazing into Mr. Gallagher's deep midnight blue eyes. The sight of him took her breath away. His dark wavy hair gleamed in the light from the entryway. He wore black jeans and a blue-and-white-striped shirt, yet his attire did not feel casual. Something about the way it hung on his large frame. Neat, streamlined, almost as if the clothes had been tailored to his body. Which they probably were. He was a very wealthy man. This house—which she could tell from the grounds and the elegant entryway behind, with the sparkling chandelier and marble floor—was clearly very expensive, and it was just one of many he owned.

But what affected her the most, standing here in front of him, was the sheer power of his presence. There was a natural air of authority about him that had nothing to do with the age difference between them.

"Ashley. Welcome."

"Thank you." She barely stopped herself from stammering the words. She hadn't realized she'd been gritting her teeth until she opened her mouth to speak, so she concentrated on relaxing her jaw.

"May I take your coat?"

She slipped off her short leather jacket and handed it to him. He opened the closet door and hung it up, then turned to her again. His gaze settled on her face, then perused lower, down her body. God, she felt underdressed in her faded jeans and lace-trimmed T-shirt. She could feel her shoulders stiffening as he examined her.

Then he smiled and some of that tension eased.

"Please, come in." He moved aside and she stepped into the large foyer.

A curved staircase led to the second story. Up there would be the bedrooms. Heat sizzled through her at thoughts of him carrying her up the stairs and tossing her onto his big bed, then stripping the clothes from her body. Her gaze darted to Mr. Gallagher and his lips curled up in amusement, as if he could read her lustful thoughts about him. A man who looked like him probably had that happen all the time.

"Would you like a tour of the house?" he asked.

She glanced back at the staircase and shook her head. "I'd love to see it, but maybe we could just talk about . . . uh . . ."

She froze. Oh, God, it was too weird to talk about this.

She'd never actually talked to him about the article. She hadn't had to because Jessica had asked a longtime friend of hers who worked at a BDSM club in town if she knew someone whom Ash could interview. Surprisingly, she'd told Jessica confidentially that Helen's stepfather, who'd just come back into town for business, frequented the club. Jessica's friend had contacted Mr. Gallagher to see if he'd be interested in being interviewed by Ashley and he'd sent her an e-mail agreeing to the interview and setting the time.

"Domination?"

The word, even coming casually from his lips, sent her insides quivering. He was a Dominant. Dom, for short. He commanded women to do as he bid. They became his sex slaves, doing whatever he wanted them to do. Her breath caught and she felt her insides melting. What would it be like to be controlled by him? For him to tell her to strip off her clothes, then get down on her knees in front of him and . . .

"Relax, Ashley. I'm not going to chain you up or anything." He smiled. "Unless you want me to."

His words evoked images of her chained to the wall, naked, his hot gaze gliding over her body. Her skin began to tingle and she felt weak-kneed.

Oh, God, this had been a terrible idea. She'd had no idea this would have such a potent effect on her.

"Follow me."

Instead of turning to the large living room off the foyer, he led her down the hallway past a formal dining room, into a casual living room off the kitchen. He sat down in a large, black leather chair. She glanced around, uncertain what to do. A bottle of red wine stood on the table, already open, and one empty stemmed glass stood beside it.

"Sit down."

Her gaze flicked to his at the tone of his words. With a slight commanding edge.

She glanced at the couch in front of him and then at the chair angled toward it.

"On the couch."

His tone brooked no argument.

She walked toward the couch and sat down.

"Thank you for agreeing to help me, Mr. Gallagher."

"You can call me Dare for now." He sat back in his chair. "I understand that you want me to teach you about Domination and submission."

"Yes, I'm doing an article for the magazine and—"

He raised his hand in a stop gesture. "A yes or no will suffice."

She stared at him, a little taken aback. His face hadn't changed at all yet somehow it seemed stern.

"I want you to understand," he said, "that we're going to do this my way."

Nervousness prickled through her. "But I have questions prepared that—"

His hard gaze stopped her flow of words instantly.

"What I intend to do is show you what a Dominant-submissive relationship is like. That's the only way you'll really understand the play of power. And the excitement."

"Um . . . but you know this is not . . . uh, I mean . . . I'd just like to clarify that . . ."

Oh, no, how did she broach this?

"Are you trying to say that you're not here for a sexual relationship?"

"Yes, that's right."

"I understand." But the twinkle in his eye didn't set her at ease.

He sat back in his chair.

"You and I have known each other for a long time," he continued, "but we don't know each other well. Still, I believe because of our shared history and the fact you and my ex-stepdaughter are good friends that you trust me."

"Yes, that's—" At his sharp expression, she stopped talking, punctuating the partial sentence with a nod.

The almost imperceptible sternness in his face softened and she felt a rush of pleasure at his approval.

"Good. That trust is very important and we're going to build on it. As we move forward you will follow my commands instantly and without question. Do you understand?"

Her chest tightened. "Yes, but . . ." Before his expression could turn to disapproval she blurted, "I mean, no." She did understand his words but she didn't *agree* with them.

He raised an eyebrow. "What is it you don't understand?"

"Well, uh . . ." She felt out of her depth. Like he was the general of a great invading force and she was a lowly peasant woman. "I need to ask questions about how things work and get background about the lifestyle and such."

"You don't learn about Domination and submission by discussing it. I think it's important that you experience it directly. So while we work on this project, you will be my sub, but we can leave out the sexual aspect, if that's what you want." He smiled, his eyes twinkling. "Personally, I think it would be better for you to have the complete experience, but you're an intelligent, perceptive and creative woman, so I am confident you can do your research to fill in that part of it."

His words of praise elated her, but the idea of being his submissive, even in a role-playing scenario meant to help her, made her insides quiver. She suspected it was as much from a blatant desire to submit to him totally as it was a resistance to being controlled. The thought of being totally under Darien Gallagher's control . . . submitting to his every whim—her heart skipped a beat—especially sexually, sent her hormones into a spin.

But that's not why she was here. She needed to stay focused on her goal and leave these disturbing urges to be examined another time.

"I don't know about this."

He gazed at her, and his inscrutable midnight eyes seemed to glow with warmth.

"You do trust me, don't you?"

When he looked at her like that—the same way he had in the past—she felt like the most important person in the world.

"Yes, of course," she replied instantly.

"Then think about why you're afraid. Is it that you're afraid of giving up your power?" He paused for a moment, watching her. "Or is it that you're afraid of coming into your power?"

She realized her jaw had clenched again and she concentrated on releasing it. Damn, how did he know her so well? Her philosophy of life was that the choices we make are often based on fear of success rather than fear of failure and we will often make choices that will sabotage what we believe we want.

She pursed her lips. She wanted to do this project. It would help her move ahead in her career. If that meant playacting with Darien Gallagher, then fine. She could do that.

"Okay. I'll do it your way."

His lips turned up in a smile. "Good."

Ashley gazed at herself in the mirror. She'd escaped to the bathroom for a few moments to collect herself. This wasn't at all what she'd expected. The intense feelings she'd had when he'd controlled how she responded to him . . . God, his authoritative tone . . . and his stern expression . . . it all took her breath away. He was so powerful and masculine.

Right now she felt like her world had turned upside down.

Dare had made a powerful case. To write an effective article about the Dominant-submissive relationship, she needed to experience it directly.

It made sense he'd show her by example, and it

wouldn't have to lead to sex. But the thought of him commanding her . . . taking control . . .

Her heart stammered.

As much as she'd insisted there would be no sexual relationship between them, she knew that she was in danger of falling under his masculine spell. That she would lose herself completely to the role of being Dare's submissive was an option that felt all too attractive right now.

Once he started to command her . . . she knew in her heart she would do anything he said.

She stared at herself in the mirror. She was thinking crazy thoughts. This was role-playing. She wasn't just going to fall into bed with him.

And he probably didn't look at her that way anyway. He was wealthy, handsome and powerful. She wasn't his type of woman.

He was just helping her with her research. Because she was a friend of Helen's.

A look of determination crossed her face. She was just looking for an excuse to run away. Because the situation was a little awkward.

She opened her purse and grabbed her brush, then pulled it through her long, dark hair.

She was going to get a grip on herself and march right back in there and get on with this.

"So how do we get started?" she asked as she sat on the couch again.

"Stand up and come over here."

At his tone, she instantly pushed herself to her feet and walked toward him.

"Good. As I told you, a submissive follows her master's commands instantly and without question."

The word *master* sent a shiver down her spine. During these sessions, Dare would be her master. He would command her to do things. She had no idea what those things would be.

"Now turn around. Slowly, so I can look at you."

She turned, aware of his gaze gliding down the length of her body. Why had she worn such tight jeans? She should have worn something more business appropriate.

What would his orders be? As she continued to turn, an image flashed through her mind of sitting on a chair in front of him, totally naked. In the image, he leaned forward and, with his gaze gliding down her torso, commanded her to open her legs.

"Stop."

She stopped turning, facing him again.

"Pour me a glass of wine."

His gaze shifted to the bottle of wine and the single stemmed glass beside it. She stepped forward and picked up the bottle, then poured the dark burgundy liquid into his glass. He held out his hand and she picked up the glass and handed it to him.

He nodded, then took a sip.

"Would you like some?"

She nodded.

"The proper response is, 'Yes, Master.'"

Her gaze darted to his. "Uh . . . yes, Master."

"Come over here and kneel in front of me."

She drew in a deep breath. A part of her wanted to rebel, but a stronger part wanted to do exactly what he said. With shaky legs, she walked toward him, then knelt on the plush carpet. She was only inches from him. His strong, masculine aura surrounded her. Exciting her. Heat pulsed through her.

He held his glass to her lips and tipped it up. She sipped the dark, tart wine, then swallowed as he drew the glass from her lips.

The wine warmed her throat as it went down.

She was so close to him. Kneeling in front of him. Being like this sent all kinds of raunchy images through her head. She found herself wondering what it would be like to stroke her hand along his thigh to his crotch. To glide her hand over his cock and feel it swell. To tug down his zipper and reach her hand inside.

"Would you like more?"

Oh, God, her raging hormones demanded so much more. But he was talking about wine.

"Yes, Master."

If she hadn't been on her knees already, she probably would have dropped to them at the intense arousal washing through her at saying those words. *Yes, Master.* Right here, right now, she was his slave.

He tipped the glass to her lips and she took a bigger sip this time. It was relaxing her and she wanted more. She glanced at him and, as if reading her mind, he tipped it up again. Heat washed through her and tension eased from her body.

She could barely keep her gaze from dropping to his crotch.

Was he aroused? If she looked, would she see a bulge forming in his pants?

If she were actually his sex slave, surely his next move would be to command her to draw out his cock and pleasure him with her mouth. To wrap her lips around the head and lick, then to glide deeper, swallowing his length inside her throat.

"Ashley, will you follow whatever command I give you right now, without question?"

Goose bumps danced across her flesh. He was going to do it.

"Yes." The word slipped from her lips before she could stop it. Her heart raced. Things were getting away from her. If he actually told her to stroke his crotch, then pull down the zipper and reach inside . . .

God, she'd do it. The way she was feeling right now, as if she totally belonged to him . . . She wanted to please him. To give him whatever he wanted.

"Good. Come closer."

She closed the few inches between them. His knee brushed against her breast as she moved and her nipples spiked. The front of the couch pressed against her body, his knees on either side of her. His long, masculine thighs open in front of her.

"Now kiss me."

She leaned forward and rested her hands on his shoulders, bringing her mouth close to his. His glowing midnight eyes watched as she moved closer. His sheer masculinity, and the feeling of power emanating from him, mesmerized her. Their lips met and sparks flashed through her. His tangy male scent filled her as their mouths merged. His lips were full and firm against hers. And warm.

She moved her mouth on his and glided her tongue along the seam of his mouth, longing to be closer. He opened and she slipped inside. His mouth was warm, and tasted of wine. The heat rushing through her was intoxicating. She deepened the kiss and his arms slid around her, pulling her tight to his body. Her heart thundered against his warm, hard chest. Her nipples tingled, jutting forward. Pressing into him.

She wanted him. If he told her to strip down right now so he could take her—thrust into her right here on the floor—she would. She *wanted* him to.

But his lips drew away. She found herself gazing into his midnight eyes, a gleam of amusement clear in those depths. Which acted like cold water splashing over her. Bringing her to her senses.

Suddenly, she felt very conscious of her position—shamelessly draped against him—and what she'd been doing. What she'd been *wanting*.

And with the evidence of her hard nipples thrusting into his chest, he knew how much she wanted him.

Oh, God, I can't believe I practically threw myself at him. But then, he'd ordered her to kiss him.

She eased back. Feeling extremely self-conscious, she retreated to the couch, needing distance between them. She sat with her ankles pressed tightly together and rested her hands on her knees.

"I thought . . ." Her words came out hoarse, so she cleared her throat. "I thought this wasn't going to be sexual. Isn't kissing crossing a line?"

"There are no lines, Ashley. I can order you to do anything."

A shiver raced through her. "But what if I don't want to do what you order?"

"Then you won't." He smiled, revealing perfect white teeth. "That's the key. You have total power over your actions. When I order you to do something, you decide whether to do it."

And she had decided to kiss him.

"Of course, if you decide not to follow a command, there will be consequences."

Her mouth went dry. "Like what?"

"I might bend you over and spank you. If you wore a dress with a thong underneath," his gaze locked on hers, "which I would like you to do from now on, I would lift up your skirt and spank your bare ass."

Her breath caught and she almost wished she'd worn a skirt today.

Shock vaulted through her at the realization she wanted him to punish her. She wanted to feel his firm hand stroke her behind, then smack it sharply.

Her head was swirling with contradictions.

If he punished her for refusing to perform a command, then she didn't really have a choice to refuse. Unless she refused to willingly accept the consequences. But what if she didn't want to be punished? Then she had no choice but to obey.

She gazed at him, confusion spiraling through her. She needed time to think about all this.

"We're done for now." Dare stood up.

She rose to her feet, too. "Okay, thank you."

She turned and headed down the hallway to the front door, then pulled on her shoes. She stood up and turned to the door. Her body tingled from his presence behind her.

"Come back tomorrow night at eight."

She stopped herself from uttering, "Yes, Master," and just nodded as she pulled open the door.

"And Ashley . . ."

She turned to look at him again. A shiver quivered through her at the warmth in those midnight eyes.

"Wear something sexy."

Ashley stared at the scrappy bit of nothing in lace that Jessica held in front of her.

"Are you kidding? I'm not going to wear that," Ashley protested.

Jessica quirked her head. "Why not?"

Ashley grabbed the tag hanging from it. Close to two hundred dollars for a tiny bodysuit composed of barely a few square inches of satin and lace.

"Because I'm not a slut."

Jessica laughed. "It's not slutty. It's sexy. And you'd look breathtaking in it." She grinned. "I mean to a man."

"To a man I'd look *breathtaking*"—Ashley said the last word with air quotes—"naked and that would be a lot cheaper."

Jessica laughed. "Well, if you're bold enough to strip down naked for him, good for you."

"Jess, stop teasing me."

"Okay, okay." Jess admired the crimson lace. "But, say what you will, I think it's worth it."

"Then you should get it," Ashley said with sincerity. She knew Jessica loved this kind of thing and she felt a little bad calling it slutty when she was just reacting to her own insecurities about the situation with Dare.

Jessica grinned. "But I'm not going out with Mr. Gallagher-the-sexiest-man-alive."

Ashley frowned. "I'm not either."

"But you are seeing him. And you asked me to help you buy sexy clothes to wear for him."

"I told you. It's not like that. And I thought you were going to stop teasing me."

"Yes, you told me and, honey . . . it *is* like that. All kidding aside, from what you told me about last night you are headed straight for an illicit, sexual affair with the man." Jessica squeezed her arm. "And I am so jealous."

Ashley's chest tightened. Leave it to Jess to give it to her straight.

"Oh, God, Jess." Ashley grabbed the hanger from Jessica and hung the garment back on the rack, her cheeks heating. Because as much as she tried to deny it . . . damn it, Jess was right.

"Come on, let's get coffee." Jessica tugged her arm, leading her from the store.

They went to the food court, then settled at a table with their coffees.

"What am I doing, Jess?" Ashley lamented over her steaming drink. "I mean, you're right. If I'm not careful, that's where this will lead."

Jess shrugged and sipped her coffee. "So why be careful? Why not seize the moment? He's handsome, worldly, and soooo sexy. And you're in this ideal situation where he'll take total control. That is so hot. You can't tell me that doesn't turn you on."

Ashley compressed her lips. "It does." She gazed straight at her friend. "Oh, God, does it ever. But how can I do that?"

"You just let him take the lead. It certainly sounds like the attraction is mutual."

"But I mean . . . he's our best friend's stepfather. And you remember how devastated Helen was when he split with her mother."

Helen had adored Dare. She'd loved that all the girls at school practically swooned over him, but more, she loved the stability he'd brought to her family. She had been without a father for a long time and when he came into the picture, she'd confessed to Ashley that she felt more secure. Ashley didn't know what the problem was— probably financial issues—because Helen always had to go home right after school to do chores. Ashley assumed it was because her mother worked late to make extra money.

"Yeah, sure, but that was years ago," Jessica said, "and, to be frank, it's not like Helen has kept up her friendship with us. We haven't heard from her in years."

When Helen's mom and Dare had divorced—the summer after graduation—Helen had dropped out of sight. She'd simply disappeared. At first, Ashley and Jessica thought she'd gone on a trip to Europe, but she'd never sent a single postcard. Then they'd heard she hadn't gone to college that fall. It was strange, since Helen had been a straight-A student and loved school.

There were all kinds of crazy rumors. Even that she'd gotten pregnant and gone away while she had the baby, then put it up for adoption. But that didn't explain why she wouldn't tell Ashley and Jessica about it. They'd been so close.

Ashley had always worried about her friend, but after the divorce, Helen's mother had moved to Cambria, a small town about a hundred miles south of Autumn's Ridge, and Dare had moved to New York, so she'd had no way to contact either of them.

"That doesn't mean we're not friends anymore," Ashley said.

Jessica raised an eyebrow. "Doesn't it?" She leaned forward. "Look, Ashley, I'm all for being loyal to a friend, but Helen walked away from us, not the other way around. As much as I loved her, we both have to face the fact that she's not our friend anymore." She squeezed Ashley's hand. "So don't you dare give up an opportunity of a lifetime for someone who can't even be bothered to keep in touch."

Wear something sexy.

Ashley couldn't believe she was dressing up in a sexy outfit to go see the man who was once her best friend's stepfather. She gulped as she stared at herself in the mirror. She couldn't believe Dare—the sexy, enigmatic man who had haunted her teenage fantasies—was now playing the role of Dom to her sub.

She inspected the black wrap-style dress she'd just put on. The black front-clasp underwire bra she wore hiked up her bosom, showing deep cleavage in the V-neckline of her dress. She wore a thong and a black garter belt to hold up her sexy black stockings. Not that she expected Dare to see any of that. Asking her to wear something sexy was part of keeping her on edge. Unsure what to expect.

And it was working like a charm.

She glanced at her watch. He'd said to arrive at eight, so she needed to leave very soon.

Tonight wouldn't get sexual. Her thoughts stirred back to the kiss they'd shared last night. The feel of his lips on hers, the taste of him on her tongue. He hadn't made a move on her, simply told her to kiss him. She had been the one who'd gotten carried away.

God, he was such a sexy man. Her heart still fluttered at the memory of being in his arms. And last night, after she'd gone to bed, she'd been filled with wicked thoughts, and steamy dreams had filled her sleep time.

But in the light of morning, she'd scolded herself. She needed to maintain her focus. This was about researching an article, not about submitting to either her desire for the man or to his sexy dominant nature. In fact, he was probably pushing her with the sexual aspect to force her to remember that she had control. Her cheeks flushed. In fact, maybe he'd been shocked at her wantonness in kissing him.

Not that Darien Gallagher was a man who was easily shocked.

Rather than disobeying his command if he ordered her to kiss him again, she could give him a chaste kiss. She fully expected that tonight he would continue to push her past her comfort zone and she'd have to decide how to follow his commands without giving in to the temptation to succumb to her lustful desires.

If she submitted to the sexual pull between them, she would be giving in to her desire to be submissive. She would be strong and avoid that.

She put on her small ruby stud earrings and headed to the door.

As she drove to his house, she felt the excitement rise in her. The pull he exerted over her was inescapable.

Dare watched Ashley's car turn into his driveway, then heard her car door close. He glanced at his watch. She was a little early. He put down his book and got up from the chair by the fire in the living room.

He'd been looking forward to this all day. Seeing Ashley again. She was delightful and sexy. Last night, he'd sported a huge erection most of the time she'd been here. Even after she'd left, it kept inflating every time he thought of her. When he'd ordered her to kiss him, it had been to see how she would react. She'd said she didn't want this to be sexual, so he had expected a protest, possibly an outright refusal, but thought it was more likely that she would give him a quick peck. He had not expected her to throw herself into it as she had, her tongue gliding into his mouth with wild abandon. And she'd clearly been turned on.

He'd meant to remain distant, but with her soft body pressed against him, her nipples hard against him, he hadn't been able to help but respond.

The doorbell rang and he smiled. He had not expected this coaching to have such delightful fringe benefits.

After she'd left, he'd struggled with the fact that taking on this role with her aroused him, especially since he was so much older—but really it was only a ten-year difference and now that she was in her late twenties, that wasn't really an issue. And, he had to admit, he'd been attracted to her all those years ago. Back then, of course, he never would have acted on it, even if he hadn't been married.

Now, however, was another matter.

Her claim that this not be a sexual situation barely fazed him. If she'd actually meant it, then he'd take it seriously, but it was so clear that she was attracted to him . . . and she was very curious about—and highly aroused by the prospect of—being his submissive and being sexually dominated by him. So much so she was practically begging for him to take her.

And if they proceeded with a sexual relationship, she probably would beg.

His lips turned up in a grin. What would it be like to be with Ashley? She'd been lovely when she was in high school, and she had grown into a stunning woman.

She might have convinced herself she only meant this interlude with him as research for her article, but that didn't mean it couldn't lead to something more. He was a good judge of people and he knew she'd been attracted to him when she was in high school. Her girlish blushes and the nervous way she'd looked away whenever he'd caught her eye had made it very clear. He wouldn't have acted on it back then, but now, with both of them adults . . . With the attraction that simmered between them, he had every intention of exploring the possibilities.

Ashley rang the bell and Dare immediately opened it.

She glanced at him nervously, worried he'd say she was late, but he simply stepped aside to let her in. She slipped off her coat and hung it up. His eyes glittered as he noticed her sexy black dress.

"Very nice."

His deep voice, smooth as silk, quivered through her. She could feel the heat of his gaze across her chest and a flush crept up her cheeks.

"Thank you. You said to wear . . . um . . . something nice."

"I *said* to wear something sexy." He smiled. "And this fits the bill quite nicely."

She stood still as he gazed at her, trying not to fidget. Finally, he turned and led her into the living room. There was a bottle of wine on the table, just like last time. She walked to it.

"Would you like me to pour you a glass?" she asked.

"Pour one for both of us." He sat down on the couch.

She filled the two stemmed glasses half full and handed him one, then turned to sit on the chair across from him.

"No, Ashley. Sit here beside me."

She hesitated, then turned and walked to the couch. She sank down beside him, extremely conscious of the heat of him beside her. His big, masculine presence made her shiver.

"What would you like to do this evening?" he asked.

"Oh, um. I want you to show me more about being a Dom."

"Of course. Everything we do will show you what our Dom-sub relationship is like. But if you were just here for a visit, what would you like to do?"

"Do you mean like talk or play games?"

"Games?" His eyes twinkled and thoughts of erotic, adult games flickered through her brain.

"Like cards or something," she quickly added.

"Yes. What would you like to spend time together doing?" He leaned back against the couch, watching her. "What do you do with your friends when you spend an evening in together?"

"Well, I have one friend. A . . . uh, a close friend . . . who comes over regularly to watch a movie."

God, she'd almost said Adam's name, but since Adam closed up whenever she asked him about his internship with Dare in college, she didn't want to mention Adam, in case there were tensions on Dare's side, too.

His eyebrow arched and his eyes seemed more solemn. "Is that your boyfriend?"

"No, we run together—for exercise, I mean—and, well . . ." She shrugged. "We're friends."

Dare sipped his drink. "But you'd like it to be more."

She frowned.

"Tell me."

She hadn't intended to. She'd been going to shrug it off. But it was as if that authoritative tone he used could get her to do anything.

"We've known each other for a while now and I am attracted to him, but he's never asked me out."

"Why wait for him to ask you? If you want to be with him, why don't you take the lead?"

She bit her lip. "I'm not good at that sort of thing."

He smiled. "That could change. As you learn more about Domination, you might like to try taking charge. Maybe you should take this opportunity to learn to be more assertive. And once you're comfortable with being in the lead, you can take control of any situation you want. At work, at home. In the bedroom."

She shivered at his words, and at the intensity of his midnight eyes.

In the bedroom was where she wanted to be with him right now. With him in control.

"So we'll watch a movie," he said.

Disappointment washed through her. How much would she learn while sitting watching a movie for two hours? On the other hand, she would be spending time with a sexy billionaire drinking expensive wine.

But she didn't really believe that Mr. Gallagher . . . Dare . . . would waste time. He was the type of man who was focused on his goals.

"Get the fourth movie on the top shelf beside the entertainment center and put it in the Blu-ray player."

She walked to the shelf and retrieved the movie, then inserted it in the device. The case was all black and she didn't recognize the name on the disc label, so she had no idea what the movie was about. She sat down beside him again as the movie started.

"I want you to sit on the floor beside me."

She put down her wineglass and stood up.

"Actually, I want you to kneel, so take off your shoes."

She sat again and crossed her legs, then unfastened the strap of her high heels. Her skirt hiked up a little and his gaze lingered on her legs.

She placed her shoes to the side, then knelt on the floor.

"Right here between my feet," he said, moving his legs apart.

She moved in front of him, then settled between his calves. He rested his hand on her shoulder as he watched the movie start up on the screen. At the warmth of his fingers cupping her shoulder, she felt a humming deep inside her. She barely saw what was happening on the screen as she found herself leaning against his knee.

He stroked her hair, his fingertips parting the strands gently as they moved. She felt like a cherished pet. She wanted to rest her head on his knee and just enjoy his attention.

Then the sound of muffled moans drew her focus to the TV.

A naked woman with a gag in her mouth was tied to a pole while a bare-chested man flicked a flogger across her back. The soft sounds she made turned to sharper cries as the man struck harder, leaving red marks on her skin.

Ashley's jaw dropped as she watched. The man pulled the gag from the woman's mouth and asked her what she wanted. She begged for him to touch her . . . to fuck her.

The man dropped his pants and held his fully erect cock in his hand, then walked toward her. Another naked man appeared and untied her, then he pushed on her back until she was bent forward. The first man pushed his cock into her mouth. The other man stepped behind her and thrust deep into her, to her moan.

Ashley turned her head away. She didn't want to watch this, especially with Dare sitting right here. Embarrassment burned through her.

"Don't you like the movie?" he asked.

"Not really."

"Call me Mr. Gallagher tonight."

Oh, God. Her embarrassment burned hotter, as if she were a teenager who'd been caught watching porn.

"Ashley, turn your head and watch the movie."

She heard the woman's moans increasing and she wanted to watch . . . to see the two men driving their cocks into her . . . then she wanted Mr. Gallagher to do the same thing to her.

But she couldn't look. Because then she'd have trouble holding back.

"No, Mr. Gallagher."

He arched an eyebrow. "You're refusing?"

She just nodded.

His expression turned stern. "I told you to watch."

She sucked in a breath, reconsidering her position, but then she shook her head.

He grasped her shoulders and stood up, pulling her to her feet with him.

"I told you there would be consequences if you disobeyed me." He marched her behind the couch then pressed on her back until she was leaning forward, just like the woman on the screen. Ashley grabbed the back of the couch to keep her balance, then . . .

She felt cold air on her ass as he flipped her skirt up out of the way. Facing this way, the screen was in front of her so she saw the three people on the screen, the woman with a cock in her mouth and another driving into her from behind.

Then she felt the sting of Mr. Gallagher's hand slapping her ass. It was . . . invigorating. He slapped again and she felt her flesh heat. His fingers glided over her behind . . . soothing . . . then his hand lifted and connected with her ass again. This time, she whimpered as he stroked her, the pain mixed with pleasure from his touch.

She found herself staring at the TV, watching the

woman pull the big cock from her mouth, her hand tightly around the base, and moan as the man behind thrust into her. The woman's eyes closed and she moaned her release.

Ashley's insides tensed and she longed for the same release.

"What do you want right now, Ashley?" Mr. Gallagher asked.

"I want you to . . ." But she bit back the rest of the sentence. She couldn't tell him she wanted him to drive into her just like the man on the screen was doing.

"Tell me," he demanded sharply.

"I want you to . . . touch me."

His hand slapped across her naked ass again. She started and turned to stare over her shoulder with wide eyes.

"That's not what you were going to say." Then his fingers stroked between her thighs and over the crotch of her panties.

Oh, God, she was soaking wet and he had to feel it. He could tell she was turned on.

"But I'll let it go this time."

He smacked her again. Then he stroked her molten folds through the silk of her panties again.

She couldn't stop her reflex to push against his hand.

His touch slid away and she felt her skirt drop back into place. Disappointment washed through her.

"Stand up."

She stood and turned to face him.

"You can refuse me. It's clear we both enjoy the consequences." His steely eyes bored into her. "But if you want this training to continue, never lie to me. Understand?"

"Yes, Mr. Gallagher," she whispered.

"That's enough for tonight. Come back in one week. In the meantime, I want you to practice what you've learned so far, but I want you to take the lead and practice being dominant. Invite your friend to help you."

"I don't think he'd want to—"

"He's your friend. He'll want to."

All Dare could think of was the feel of Ashley's soft round ass in his hand, her skin heated from his spanking. He shouldn't have stroked between her legs. The feel of her wetness nearly drove him over the edge. He'd wanted nothing more than to sink his hard, throbbing erection into her sweet, melting heat.

But he'd held back.

The sight of her desire-filled eyes had almost been his undoing, though. She clearly loved him touching her and she would have begged him to fuck her if he'd pushed it.

And maybe he should have. But it just felt wrong. Not because he was older, or because she was friends with his ex-stepdaughter. Ash was an adult now—his cock twitched as he thought about her shapely body—but she had come to him for guidance, not for a sexual tryst.

She was new to this. Vulnerable to her own newly dis-covered desires. And, as much as he'd like to fulfill those desires, he didn't want to take advantage of her.

So he'd sent her on her way. Even suggested she prac-tice with this man she was interested in. If he reciprocated Ashley's feelings . . . feelings she was too shy to express . . . then Dare had done them both a favor, because Ash cared for this man and wanted more from their relationship, so surely when pushed into this situation, the man would be able to sense Ash's need.

Dare understood it wasn't necessarily him that Ash wanted. She just wanted a strong man to show her what it was like to be dominated.

He hoped the other man was up to it.

He sat on the couch and wrapped his hand around his aching cock, thinking of Ashley's warm wetness against his fingers.

Fuck, who was he kidding? He hoped the man choked and that Ash came back to Dare even needier. He stroked his cock. Then maybe he'd get over his heroism and just give her what she wanted.

What they both wanted.

"So how is it going?" Adam asked as he ran alongside Ashley.

She'd been different this past week since she'd started this research of hers. More reserved.

"Fine."

He chuckled. "That's it? Fine? You're role-playing a Dom-sub relationship with a strange man and you just say it's fine."

She pursed her lips and nodded.

He hated the fact that she seemed uncomfortable talking to him about it.

"Was it awkward?"

"No, not awkward."

"So he explains stuff to you?" he asked, wanting her to talk about what happened in these sessions.

"Um, yeah. Sort of."

"Surely you can give me more than that. I'm interested in how it's going."

She gazed at him as they ran along the path through the park.

"That's good, because I have a favor to ask."

"Sure, what is it?"

"Well, Dare thinks I should ask you to help me practice."

He grinned. "I could do that."

This could work out perfectly. What a great way to get insight into what went on during her training. And even better, it would give him a chance to spend time with her. And maybe give her a taste of his own brand of domination.

"Wait, what did you say about a dare?" he asked.

Her eyes widened and she shook her head. "Oh, nothing."

"Ash . . ."

"I just mentioned his name. It's Dare."

His eyes narrowed. "What's his last name?"

But this couldn't be the same Dare. The man he'd known in college. The man who'd . . . Just the thought made his chest so tight he could barely breathe. He slowed down and headed to a nearby bench and sat down to collect himself. Ash followed him.

He really hoped it wasn't the same Dare. That man was only five or six years older than Adam. And he was wealthy and exceptionally good-looking. He only had to look at a woman with his compelling navy eyes and they melted into a puddle at his feet.

Ashley sat beside him. "I . . . didn't want to mention

it but . . . the man who's helping me with my research is Darien Gallagher. I didn't mean to let his name slip."

Fuck!

Hearing that name again was like a punch to the gut.

"Why?" he asked. Did she know about what had happened?

"Well, when I asked you about your internship with him, you always closed up, so I figured there was some tension between the two of you. I thought it was better just not to mention it."

Tension was an understatement. The man had torn his life to shreds.

And now he was afraid that he'd do it again by stealing Ashley away from him.

Adam sat on the chair kitty-corner to the couch while Ash disappeared into the kitchen. This evening would be . . . interesting, to say the least. Ash was going to practice her Domme skills on him.

Ashley walked toward him with a bottle of wine and two glasses, which she placed on the table near the couch and sat down. She glanced his way uncertainly.

"You don't have to be nervous," he said. "It's just me."

Her head bobbed up and down in a nod. "I know. I just . . . I'm not sure how to get started."

"Okay, well, what did your mentor do?"

She'd already explained that Dare was teaching her by example, which made Adam nervous because he was certain it wouldn't be long before Dare started commanding her to do intimate, erotic things. Ash had insisted it wasn't like that. Not that he'd asked, but she'd felt the need to explain it.

But the man was only human and Ash was . . . well, she was sweet and a little timid . . . and delightfully sexy. She was any Dom's dream. It had to be wildly exciting to have her sitting in front of him, ready and willing to submit to his will.

Adam was getting hard just thinking about it.

"Um . . . well, he asked me what I wanted to do." She bit her lip. "I think . . . you know . . . because he wanted to take an everyday situation and show me how he could . . . you know . . . how it could turn into a Dominant-submissive situation."

"What did you tell him?"

"I said I like to watch movies with you. That's why he knows about you and suggested I practice with you."

"He knows about me?" How much did he know? Just that he was Ash's friend, or that he and Dare already knew each other?

Her cheeks turned pink. "Well, not *you*. Just that you're my friend and we run together. And watch movies."

"He thought I was your boyfriend." That's why she was acting off.

She nodded. "But I set him straight. That we're just friends."

Adam wanted their relationship to be more, but he took heart from her reaction. If she really thought of him as just a friend, with no romantic prospects, she wouldn't be so flustered.

"All right. So we watch a movie." He stood up and walked toward the TV.

"Wait, what are you doing?" she asked.

He turned to her. "I'm going to put on a movie."

"No, but . . . that ruins it. I need to . . . you know . . . order you to do it."

He grinned. "Okay, sorry." He sat back in the chair. "And are you going to order me to strip down to my boxers first?"

Her eyes widened, then she glanced away. "No, of course not."

Idiot, he chided himself.

"Sorry, Ash. I was just kidding. Go ahead."

"Um, okay. Well, first, pour us some wine."

He reached for the bottle. She'd already loosened the cork so he pulled it free and poured the rosé into the two glasses.

"Good, and when you do something . . ." She frowned. "I mean when I tell you to do something, then answer with 'yes' . . . um . . . I guess 'Mistress.'"

He smiled. "Really?"

She tipped her head. "I'm sorry. You think this is really silly. We don't have to do this." She stood up, clearly ready to herd him out the door.

"No, it's okay, I'll behave." He grinned again. "Unless you want to punish me?"

Her gaze darted to him, then she giggled nervously.

Fuck, his cock lurched at the realization that the thought excited her. And it was quite possible that punishment had worked into her scenario with Dare the other night.

"Ash, let's just walk through exactly what you did with your mentor."

She nodded, then drew in a deep breath.

"Walk to the TV and retrieve the movie sitting on the shelf above the Blu-ray player, then put it in the machine."

"Yes, Mistress."

He stood and retrieved the movie. It was a romantic comedy. Chick flick all the way. He put it in the player, then returned to the chair.

"Over here by me," she said patting the couch beside her.

He smiled. "Yes, Mistress." He sat down beside her.

"Now take off your shoes."

He glanced at his sock-clad feet. "I took my shoes off when I came in."

"Oh, right. Good. So now, I want you to kneel in front of me."

He sank to the floor and knelt in front of her. They were eye-to-eye and she gazed at him in surprise.

"No, I mean . . . uh . . . the other way. I want you to kneel in front of me while we watch the movie."

"If I turn, my feet will bump your ankles."

"Right." She opened her legs, then quickly pulled at her skirt to cover her exposed undies, but too late. He'd caught a seductive glimpse of baby blue lace.

He turned and knelt in front of her, but he kept his legs straight rather than sitting on his calves, knowing that he was blocking her view.

She rested her hand on his shoulder, sending heat rolling through him. She stroked, but then pushed down a little. He purposely didn't take the hint.

"Um . . . I want you to . . ." She pushed down. "Can you kneel down more?"

"Yes, Mistress."

He bent his legs, then leaned back a little, feeling her silky thighs on either side of him. Fuck, this was torture, but the *oh, so good* kind.

Her fingers stroked through his hair, sending ripples of awareness through him. He wanted to lean back and rest his head against her breasts. To enjoy her gentle caresses over his hair while he gazed up at her lovely face.

Then he wanted to turn and drag her into his arms and consume her mouth, then press her back onto the couch and prowl over her.

"Oh, this isn't working. You must be bored stiff."

He had to stifle a chuckle. He certainly was stiff, but not because he was bored.

"I don't know what I'm doing," she lamented.

"Ash, I'm not bored, and I'm happy to do whatever you need. Just relax. What did you do the other night with him? Did you watch the whole movie?"

"No. I . . . didn't like the movie. I think he picked something to purposely push me to disobey. He wants me to understand that it's okay to refuse if I'm uncomfortable."

"That's good. So you protested?"

"Yes. I mean, sort of. I stopped watching it."

He turned to face her. "What did he do when you disobeyed? Did he punish you?"

She bit her lip and nodded.

Fuck, he wanted to ask if Dare had exposed her naked ass. If he'd cupped her round flesh in his hand then smacked it until it stung. But the flush on her cheeks assured him that's what had happened.

She lifted her gaze to his, then her blue eyes widened. His smile had faded and she must have known that he was wildly turned on. God, he could barely resist his deep yearning to kiss her. Her lips looked so velvety soft and . . . his body tightened . . . would they part for his tongue? At the thought of slipping it inside her warm mouth, the ache inside him blossomed to intense need. He could imagine her tongue gliding over his, then she would open wider as he deepened the kiss.

He wanted to slide his arms around her and draw her close. To feel her soft breasts pressed tight to him and . . . oh, fuck, the tight buds of her nipples boring into him. He longed to stroke one. He wanted to feel the hard nub against his thumb. And to hear her whimpers of pleasure as he teased her to a delicious state of arousal.

Suddenly, he realized he'd actually started leaning in toward her. Her eyes were wide, watching him.

Fuck, what the hell was he doing?

He drew back and stared into her dazed eyes.

"Let's get back to you practicing your domination," he said.

"Of course."

He glanced briefly at the TV, then back to her. "So, Mistress, what if I tell you I don't want to watch the movie?"

"I order you to watch it," she said firmly.

"And if I refuse?" The words just slipped out.

"I'll have to punish you, then," she said, looking nervous.

His cock hardened at the thought that she might slap his ass. The thought of her small, feminine hand connect-

ing with his hard ass—God, would she tell him to drop
his pants?—sent his hormones reeling.

It was too much. He needed to feel her against him.

He cupped her face in his hands and drew her close.
She tipped up her head and her lips brushed his.

The mere touch of her softness against his mouth made
his cock swell even more. Then she pressed her tongue
into his mouth and he moaned. Passion flared between
them and he clutched her tightly to his body. Her lips
moved seductively on his and by the time their mouths
parted, he was totally off balance.

"Fuck, Ash. That was some kiss."

She smiled, her eyes full of desire. "You don't know
how long I've waited for you to do that."

"Look, Ash. That was just a mistake. We can't go
down this path."

"But . . . why not?"

"How many reasons do you want? I'm older than you,
I'm your brother's friend—"

"I don't care about the age difference. And you and
Brad haven't been close since he moved to San Diego. You
and I are closer friends now."

He frowned. "And I'm your boss."

She wrapped her arms around his neck. "That doesn't
matter."

"It does. Things will get complicated. It'll get awkward at work."

He took her wrists and disentangled himself from her
arms.

"I'm sorry, Ash. This is just a really bad idea."

•   •   •

Ashley climbed into bed, still stinging from Adam's rejection. She was sure he'd been as affected by that kiss as she had.

She might not have been sure about his interest in her back when she was younger, but she was pretty sure that she'd seen simmering interest in his eyes sometimes when they were together. Like that one time when she went to his place for a swim and she wore that extra skimpy bikini. She had seen a very masculine reaction. She had almost thought he would make a move on her.

Jessica's theory was that Adam was gay, and he just kept his relationships under wraps. Ashley didn't understand why he would—people in Autumn's Ridge were pretty accepting—but then she didn't really buy into the theory. And especially not now, after that kiss.

She pulled the covers around her. He'd given her reasons. The age thing, his friendship with her brother, the fact that he was her boss. But she believed there was more going on than that.

She knew something had happened when he was in college—some relationship gone wrong—and he'd been hurt. Badly.

In the two years she'd worked for him, she'd never known him to date. At least, he never told her about it if he did. Which was odd because they talked about almost everything else in their lives. Could that have something to do with why he resisted their mutual attraction?

If only she could get him to open up about it.

Ashley sank back in her chair as she watched Jessica poke at her dinner. Jess was trying to eat healthier, and had invited her over to try a new recipe. She was testing fish dishes, and the salmon had been delicious.

"Don't you like it?" Ashley asked.

"Oh, no. I do." Jess took the last bite, then pushed her plate aside. "I'm just a bit distracted. It's been a busy week."

"Problems?" Ashley knew that Jessica loved her job as the buyer for a trendy clothing boutique, but she also knew that politics and creative differences with the manager sometimes frustrated Jess.

Jess glanced her way. "At work? No, everything's fine."

Ashley sipped her wine.

"Okay, if everything at work's fine, then what's bothering you?"

Jess sighed and stood up, picking up her plate. Ashley did the same and helped clear the table, then carried the dishes into the kitchen. Jess squirted dish soap in the sink and turned on the water. Bubbles danced across the surface as the sink filled.

"It's not that there's anything bothering me," Jess said, "but I wanted to tell you something."

"Oh? What's that?"

Jess placed the dishes in the sink and started washing them. Jess grabbed a tea towel and picked up a wineglass, then wiped it dry.

"Well, I friended Dare Gallagher on Facebook."

Ashley dried a plate. "Why?"

Jess shrugged. "I don't know. I've done that with parents of other friends. You know, just to see how they're doing and keep in touch. I didn't know if he would remember me, but we did used to hang out at his house with Helen a lot in high school."

Ashley smiled. "I'm sure he still remembers you." She leaned against the counter. "But I bet what you wanted was to see if he was posting anything about me and him."

Jess nodded. "Yeah, I guess. Not that I thought he'd be overt about it, but he might say something. And maybe there'd be some clue about other relationships. And photos."

Ashley smiled. "So you wanted to see if there are any hot pictures of him."

"Guilty."

"And I think you're being a bit of a softy. I bet you were hoping there might be some photos with him and Helen, or her mom. Or maybe that they're talking on Facebook." Ashley grabbed another plate and dried it. "Even though you claim that it doesn't bother you that we've lost touch with Helen, I think you were hoping to see how she's doing."

Jess unplugged the sink and, as the water drained away, she started putting away the dishes Ashley had set on the counter.

Jess pursed her lips. "If that's the case, then why don't you think I'd just friend Helen?"

Ashley squeezed her arm and smiled. "Because I know you and I get that you don't want to be the first to break the silence between the two of you. Requesting to be her friend would make you vulnerable if she refused."

Ashley realized that Jess had also made herself vulnerable to Dare's rejection.

"Oh, Jess, is that what happened with Dare? Did he refuse your friend request?"

"No, he actually accepted."

"That's good." Ashley was glad Dare hadn't rejected

her friend. She grabbed a cloth and wiped the counter as Jess put the leftovers in the fridge.

"So, did you find anything interesting on his page?"

This time Jess smiled. "You mean, did I find anything about you?" She laughed. "No, not a thing. So that's good."

True, Ashley was glad he wasn't spreading it around that she was being his submissive, or that he was training her—that would be so embarrassing—but, of course, he wouldn't. It would be nice, though, if he'd mentioned something about having met an interesting woman or started an interesting project, or anything at all that referred to what they were doing.

But, of course, she was just being silly. Saying nothing was the best course.

And she knew Darien Gallagher was a very private man. In a way, she was surprised he even had a Facebook page. But in this day and age, of course he would.

Jess grabbed a second bottle of wine and opened it, then poured two glasses. Ashley followed her into the living room and sat down.

"The thing is," Jess said, "shortly after that, I got a friend request from Helen."

Shock shimmered through Ashley.

"Really? That's surprising . . . but it's great that she's in touch with you again. It's quite a coincidence."

Jess lounged back on the couch, the full wineglass in her hand.

"Actually, I don't think so. I think she saw that I became friends with Dare and that prompted her to contact me."

"Contact you?"

"Well, yes. After I friended her, she sent me a message." Jess sipped her wine.

"What did she say?"

"She told me that she'd heard Dare was in town for a couple of months working on a business deal and asked if I'd run into him. I told her no."

A chill ran through Ashley. "You didn't say anything about the fact that he and I . . . uh . . ." She bit her lip. "Well, of course, I know you wouldn't."

"No, I didn't say anything about you and him. Not even that you've seen him. Especially since I don't know why she was so interested in whether I'd seen him or not, or that I'm connecting with him at all."

Ashley plumped up the pillow behind her, then leaned back.

"I think you're reading more into it than there is. She probably just saw that he friended you and it made her think it would be nice to connect with you again."

A part of Ashley was jealous that Helen hadn't thought to contact Ashley, too. Helen and Ashley had been best friends for years before Jessica moved to town when they were in their early teens.

Ever since Ashley's mom had died when she was eight, her dad had always pushed her to watch out for herself. To keep her emotions in check and deal with them on her own. Not to depend too much on anyone. But sometimes, she'd needed to talk to someone about her feelings. And Helen had always been there for her. She had understood Ashley's pain.

But when Jessica showed up, suddenly Jessica and Helen had been best buddies and Ashley had felt like an outsider. Not that they hadn't included her, but the two of them seemed to share so much more. Jessica was always willing to try new things and push the limits, getting them all into trouble more than once. That fascinated Helen, who wanted to break free of her nerdy, smart-girl image and become more popular. Then the year before graduation, it was Helen who seemed to be the one looking for trouble. Near the end, she seemed to pull back from both of them. That was when Jessica and Ashley became closer.

But now that Helen was in touch with Jessica again, Ashley felt really left out.

Dare parked his car, then walked to the bench facing the small pond in the park where Ashley had asked to meet him. She was already sitting there, throwing small chunks of bread to some ducks. She glanced up as he approached.

She'd told him on the phone that she wanted to talk to him outside of their sessions. He suspected she wanted to end their mentoring. She probably found dealing with her newly discovered arousal at being punished a little too difficult to deal with.

He was determined to talk her into continuing.

"Thanks for coming," she said as he sat down beside her.

"Of course. What did you want to talk about?"

She compressed her lips. "You're always very direct, aren't you?"

"It keeps things simple."

She nodded and threw a few more crumbs to the birds, then put the bag on the bench beside her.

"I wanted to talk to you about . . . uh . . . well, when

we're together, there seems to be . . ." She bit her lip, then drew in a breath. "You remember that first time when I said that there shouldn't be anything sexual between us?"

"Yes, I do. And I've been using that to push you to set limits so you understand the power you have even as a submissive."

"But the result is that . . ." She fidgeted with the tie on the bottom of her jacket. "Well, you could tell that what you were doing was . . . exciting to me."

He smiled. "Yes, I could."

"So, I'd like us to find a way to continue the role-playing but stay away from anything sexual."

"Why?"

She started, gazing at him with wide eyes. "Uh . . . it would make me more comfortable."

"Ash, you're not doing this to be comfortable. You're doing it to explore something new and different. Something that excites you."

"It's just research for an article," she replied.

"No, it's more than that. You're curious about what it would be like to be in a Dom-sub relationship. A *sexual* relationship. And that scares you. Because it pushes you outside your comfort zone."

He reached his hand in front of her and she leaned back against the wooden bench, clearly thinking he was going to pull her into his arms, but he picked up the bag of bread and threw some to the ducks lingering near the bench.

"Ash, it's not my fault that you're aroused by the Dom-sub situation. If you weren't, I wouldn't push in that direction, but you clearly are."

"But that doesn't mean we have to go in that direction."

He chuckled. "We don't have to. But you want to. And you want me to push you."

"No, I don't." Uncertainty laced her words.

He turned to her, locking his gaze with her wide blue eyes. "Ash, I told you not to lie to me."

She straightened up, gazing at him uncertainly.

"I believe the idea of exploring a sexual relationship with me . . ." he continued, "where I dominate you completely . . . exhilarates you. I think you want to pursue it more than anything." He leaned in closer. "Where I command you to do sexy things to me. Like telling you to strip off your clothes and kneel in front of me. To pull out my cock and take it in your mouth, then suck it until I come in your mouth."

His breath lightly brushed her neck, sending tingles dancing along her skin.

His voice became a low, husky growl. "Where I push you against the wall and take you hard and fast."

When he stroked a wisp of hair from her face, she sucked in a breath, her wide eyes glowing with desire.

He brushed his lips against her temple. "Tell me I'm wrong."

Ashley sucked in air, staring at his intense midnight eyes, her body trembling from the light brush of his lips. The moment he'd sat down beside her, her heartbeat had accelerated and she'd found it increasingly difficult to breathe. Just being close to him made her a crazy mess of need, and the thought of him dominating her sent tremors of excitement through her.

He was absolutely right. She wanted to explore these new feelings. To be controlled by him and taken to a new realm of eroticism.

"You see, you can't. So what do you want to do? Do you want to end our sessions?"

"No, I don't. I . . ."

"So tell me what this is really about."

She exhaled. "It's just that . . . you're the stepfather of my friend and I don't think she'd like it if something happened between us."

"*That's* what's bothering you? First, Helen is no longer my stepdaughter. Hasn't been for years. And how long has it been since you've interacted with her?"

"Sure, but—"

"No buts. Ash, you can't let what other people want—or what you think they want—dictate what you do. If you want something, go after it. Whether it's the friend you want a romantic relationship with, or having an illicit sexual experience with me."

Her lips turned up in a smile. "Illicit?"

He laughed. "Well, that does make it sound more exciting, doesn't it?"

She gazed into his eyes, feeling herself caught up in the deep blue depths.

"Everything about you is exciting."

A smile crept across his face, wide and devastatingly sexy.

Oh, God, she couldn't believe she'd said that out loud.

He took her hand and stood up. "Come with me."

"Where are we going?" she asked as he led her along the path through the trees toward the road.

"We're going back to my place."

"But . . ."

He stopped and turned. With her forward momentum, she collided with his body.

His big, hard, muscular body.

His hands grasped her arms, then his lips captured hers. She pushed onto her tiptoes, needing to be closer. Needing to feel his lips pressing harder on hers. His tongue swept into her mouth and she murmured softly. He took her mouth with passion, consuming her. But then the kiss softened, becoming almost tender. His arms slid around her and he drew her closer, like a cherished lover, while he seduced her mouth with his talented lips.

She melted against him, her heart beating frantically, feeling the echo of his own heartbeat against her.

Then he drew away, his solemn gaze locked on hers.

"You have a choice at every step of the way, but know that when I get you home, I am going to tear away every one of your barriers and build up your need to a fever pitch, then I am going to take full advantage of the situation and take you to a place you've never been before. And I warn you, you will quickly lose the will to say no. So decide carefully before you say you'll come with me."

He stared at her, waiting.

She should say no. She should walk away right now.

But "should" was a word she resisted. It was self-limiting and hinted at externally imposed barriers. Because she could do anything she wanted. The only one who had a right to dictate what she did or didn't do was her.

And what she wanted to do . . . what the overwhelming desire burning inside her insisted she do . . . was go with him. She wanted to submit to him. To be vulnerable to him.

To trust in him and give herself to him in every way.

As soon as the door closed behind them, Dare swept Ashley into his arms and kissed her. She melted against him, the heat of the desire that had been building on the drive there filling her with anticipation.

Then he drew away. She could see only a flicker of the heat in his eyes as he schooled his expression to one of calm authority.

"You will do everything I say to the letter. You will not argue or hesitate. Do you understand?"

"Yes, sir."

"Sir. I like that. You will address me as Mr. Gallagher or sir. Follow me."

He led her to the stairway, then up to the second floor. Through double doors at the end of the hall she caught a glimpse of a big, four-poster bed in deep mahogany. She followed him toward it, but then he stopped at a door on the right and opened it. He turned on a light, casting away the darkness, and led her inside. She glanced around, her eyes widening at the rough-hewn wooden furniture around the room: a large, X-shaped piece in one corner, about seven feet tall, with cuffs attached. Padded benches of different shapes, all with restraints. And a tall cupboard along one wall.

And a bed on one side, covered with black sheets.

He led her to a large chair and sat down. She stood waiting uncertainly.

"Come here."

She stepped toward him.

"Unbutton your shirt."

He wanted her to undress? Oh, God, this was becoming all too real, all too fast.

But she obeyed. Her fingers moved to the top button and she unfastened it. Then to the second. Her skin flushed as her shirt slowly opened, revealing a glimpse of her bare skin and lacy bra beneath.

When she'd finished with the bottom button, she slid her hands up the placket, ready to open the blouse, but he took her hands and drew her close.

"Do only what I say and no more," he said, his voice matter-of-fact.

He placed her hands at her sides, then he slowly parted her shirt, revealing her lace-clad breasts. The heat of his gaze seared her as he stared at her swelling breasts, the nipples pushing at the thin lace. He slid the shirt over her shoulders and it glided down her arms and fell to the floor.

His hands glided up her ribs, then under her breasts, and one thumb glided over her hard nub. Her breath caught at the incredible sensations vibrating through her. Then his other thumb brushed over her second nipple and she thought her knees would buckle.

"Turn around."

She turned, and once her back was to him, she felt his fingers work at the hooks of her bra. Then it released. He slid the straps off her shoulders and she let the bra follow her shirt to the floor.

"Now turn toward me."

Oh, God, when she turned he would see her naked from the waist up. She felt vulnerable and uncertain.

But she turned.

And when she did, the admiration in his eyes as he gazed at her full breasts filled her with delight. She wanted to run her hands underneath them and lift. To move closer and offer them to him.

"You have beautiful breasts. Do you like me looking at them?"

"Yes, Mr. Gallagher."

He smiled. "Good."

He wrapped his hands around her waist and drew her closer then, with one hand on the small of her back, he cupped her breast with the other. The heat of his big, masculine hand around her sent her hormones swirling. Then he leaned forward and covered the aureole with his mouth. His tongue nudged the hard nipple . . . then he sucked.

"Ohhh," she moaned.

He lapped and suckled for a few more minutes before moving to the other. When he took that in his hot mouth, she moaned again.

"Now take off your jeans."

She undid the snap, then drew down the zipper. She watched his hot gaze as she pushed them down her hips and let them drop to the floor. She stepped out of them and kicked them to the side.

"Turn around."

She turned her back to him, conscious of his heated gaze lingering on her bare behind.

She felt his lips on her. They fluttered over her round flesh in butterfly kisses. So delicate and sexy. Then his fingertips grazed the flimsy fabric of her panties, brushing against her melting folds.

Oh, God, she thought she'd die. This was so intensely intimate.

His fingers glided under the elastic lace of the thong and he drew it downward. Soon, he'd peeled away the last bit of cloth covering her naked body. He pressed his hand against her back and eased her forward until she was bent over.

He was looking at her. She could feel it. Gazing at her intimate folds.

Then she jumped as she felt his mouth touch her. His tongue pressed into her folds and he licked her.

He pressed her thighs apart, opening her to him, then his tongue pushed deeper into her. His hand returned to her back and he pressed her down further, then his mouth covered her. He found her clit and teased it.

"Oh, yes."

"Do you like that?"

"Yes, Mr. Gallagher."

His fingertip brushed her clit. She choked back a moan as it quivered over the tiny bud. Pleasure rippled from that spot to her very core.

He licked her again as his fingers dipped into her. Just a little. Teasing.

Then they slipped away. So did his mouth.

"Ashley, come stand in front of me."

She stood up and turned to face him.

He tucked his hands under her breasts and lifted, gazing at each one. He caressed them gently. Sparks flared from her nipples to her inner core.

"That feels so good, Mr. Gallagher."

He leaned forward and licked her nipple, suckled for a moment, driving her wild, then lapped at the other. When he drew away, abandoning her needy breasts, she moaned in disappointment.

"Now it's time for you to do something for me."

"Anything, sir."

He smiled. "Kneel down."

She knelt, conscious of the growing bulge in his pants.

"Undress me."

"Yes, sir."

She started with the top button of his shirt and unfastened it, catching a glimpse of hard muscle beneath. That expanded as she undid the second, then the third. When she had all the buttons undone, she ran her hands up his stomach, then over his chest, delighting at the feel of his rock-hard, sculpted muscles under her fingertips.

She pushed the shirt off, then her gaze dropped to his pants. She unfastened the button, then grasped the zipper tab and pulled it down. Slowly. Inside, she could see his thick, swollen cock straining at the light cotton of his briefs. He stood up, his body moving closer to her, and pushed down his pants. Then he waited, his briefs still covering— barely—his distended cock.

She tucked her fingers under the elastic and drew them down, slowly. Her gaze locked on the exposed head of his cock, then the long shaft as she drew down the fabric. She pushed the briefs down his thick thighs to the floor, then gazed up at his long, hard cock, pointing straight to the ceiling.

Maybe it just appeared so incredibly long because she was looking up at it, but when she straightened up and he sat down, she found herself gazing at it close-up and her eyes widened.

"Oh, my God. It's so big."

He chuckled. "True." Then he leaned forward and pressed his lips to her ear. "And soon it will be inside you."

The softly spoken words swirled into her ear and she sucked in a breath. Yes, she wanted that. So badly.

"Now suck it," he said.

"Yes, sir," she murmured, mesmerized by the sight of his monumental shaft.

She wrapped her hand around the base, barely able to get her fingers around it, then leaned forward and pressed her lips to his tip.

It was his turn to moan, a soft, yet masculine utterance.

She dragged her tongue over him, tasting the salty droplet glistening near the small opening on the crown. Then she swept her tongue over him again.

She opened her mouth and took his mushroom-shaped head inside her mouth. Twirling her tongue under the ridge, she delighted in the sound of his murmurs of approval.

Her hand stroked up and down his hard shaft as she teased his cockhead, listening to his rapid breathing. She glided downward, taking as much of his length as she could, then slid up again, her hand following. He watched her, his eyes burning with desire.

Her other hand glided downward until she felt his soft

sacs, then she cupped them. She kept her gaze locked on his as she fondled his balls while his cock glided in and out of her mouth. His cock twitched and she could feel the sacs tightening. Soon she would make him come. Feel the pulsing of his cock as he came in her mouth. And she would swallow every drop.

His hand coiled in her hair and he guided her at his desired pace. Up and down. Pushing his thick cock a little deeper each time, until she believed she would somehow swallow him whole. His member throbbed in her mouth, his balls hard as walnuts.

Then he stopped, and drew her mouth away from his erection. He sat for a moment, watching her as he seemed to struggle with regaining control of his body. Then he stood up and guided her across the room. She was sure he was taking her to the bed, but instead he stopped at a tall bench with chains hanging from the ceiling. He clamped leather straps around each of her wrists—the restraints nicely cushioned inside—then pulled a cord, which tugged her arms over her head. He sat her on the padded bench.

"Legs wide," he instructed.

She opened her legs, resting her heels on a lip probably designed for that purpose.

Here she was, totally naked in front of him, her breasts heaving with her excitement, her thighs spread wide and him gazing at her glistening folds.

He knelt in front of her and his mouth pressed against her dampness. When he suckled her clit, she cried out.

His fingers glided inside her and she moaned. He stroked her passage, eliciting an intensely compelling desire that demanded satiation. She needed him to show her the way to ecstasy.

He locked gazes with her. "What do you want, Ash?"

She gasped. His fingers quivering inside her had dragged her to the brink and now . . . she shivered as pleasure swelled . . . now she was going to . . .

"Ohhh, yesss!"

His eyes glowed as he moved his fingers inside her, watching her intently.

Her eyelids fluttered closed as the sensations burst through her, exploding in an earth-shattering orgasm. She cried out in ecstasy, losing herself in the maelstrom of pleasure.

As she floated back to earth, his lips found hers, his tongue pushing gently into her mouth. It pulsed inside her and she sucked on it, pulling it deeper until he moaned.

His hands glided down her naked back and she became aware of her breasts pushed tight to the hard muscles of his chest.

"What do you want, Ash?" he asked again.

"You," she whispered. "Inside me."

"Fuck." He stood up and drew her to the edge of the bench. Then she felt it. His hot, hard flesh brush against her slick, steaming opening. So wet, he would slide right in.

"Please, I want you now."

He nuzzled her ear. "Tell me you want me to fuck you."

"Oh, yes, Mr. Gallagher. I want you to fuck me. I've wanted that for so long. Pleeeaaase fuck me!"

On a low groan, he eased forward.

She could see in his eyes that he was using every shred of control he possessed to glide into her slowly. His cock was thick and hard, stretching her. Almost painfully, he was so big. But she wanted him. Wanted it. All the way. Filling her like no man had ever filled her before.

Still he glided. Only halfway in.

"Oh, God, yes. It feels so good."

That was too much for him and he drove deep. She gasped. Tears prickled in her eyes at the sweetness of the pleasure-pain of having him fully immersed in her body.

"Yes," she whimpered, then squeezed him inside.

He moaned in response.

"Please, Mr. Gallagher. Please fuck me now."

"God damn." He drew back, then thrust deep again.

She felt the tears flow from her eyes. The sensations were so incredibly . . . sweetly . . . explosive.

"Yes," she whimpered again. "Fuck me."

He groaned and drew back, then drove deep again. He kept filling her. His big, long cock dragging along her tender inner passage, then pulsing deep again. In. Out. Faster and faster. His hand on the small of her back, steadying her as he drove into her like a piston.

Her hands wrapped around the chains above her to steady herself and she wrapped her legs around his waist. His next thrust drove even deeper and she cried out. Her grip tightened on the chains.

He buried his face in her hair as he drove into her fast and hard.

"You feel so fucking good around me, baby."

She could only utter a soft moan.

"I'm going to fucking come so hard." His lips grazed her ear. "But not until you do."

Then he slammed hard into her body. She gasped as an orgasm blossomed deep inside her and exploded outward, thundering through her body in a massive, ecstatic eruption of joy. She wailed at the top of her lungs, riding the wave of ecstasy, clinging to the chains, her legs clenching around him in a death grip.

Then he groaned and erupted inside her. She gasped at the feel of his hot seed filling her and shuddered in another orgasm. Then faded into blackness.

Ashley jerked awake. She didn't know if seconds or minutes had passed, but she found herself on the bed with the black sheets. She gazed up to see Dare's face, his expression filled with concern.

"Are you okay?" he asked.

She wrapped her arms around his neck and stared at him in awe. "That was incredible."

He chuckled. "Well, I have to admit, that's the first time I made a woman faint."

She laughed, feeling delightfully giddy. "Feel free to do it again anytime."

He laid down beside her and drew her against his naked body. "Believe me. I will."

Ashley sipped her glass of wine as she and Dare sat on the deck in his backyard watching the sunset. She couldn't believe she'd just had the most incredible sex of her life with this incredibly gorgeous, older man just a half hour ago. God, he was her best friend's stepfather. And now they were just sitting here drinking wine together.

He seemed to take it all in stride, but she was a quivery mess, just trying to keep a calm exterior while they spent this quiet time together. What she really wanted, though, was for him to command her to strip and do it all over again.

"Do you want to talk about it?" Dare asked.

Her gaze darted to his. "What?"

"We just took our relationship from a mentor arrangement to a full-fledged Dominant-submissive sexual relationship."

"Relationship?"

"I use the word loosely. We may want things to stay casual between us, but this kind of Dom-sub relationship can be complicated so we need to be sure we both understand where things are and where they're going."

"Where are they going?" she asked.

"I assume we'll continue this as long as I'm in town." He smiled. "We both certainly seem to enjoy it."

She felt her cheeks heat, but she nodded. "And once you leave?"

He frowned. "Ash, I don't see this becoming a long-term thing. You know I'm only here for another month or so, then once my business is finished, I go back to New York. And you have your job here. I don't think either of us wants to complicate things by assuming there's a future for us."

She nodded. "Of course." It sounded so reasonable, but she still felt unwanted.

"So are you happy about the information you're getting for your article?" he asked.

She pursed her lips. Better to think about that than wallow in her feelings of rejection.

She nodded. "But I wanted to do one post with tips on being a Dominant, and one on being a sub, but so much of what you do seems to be a part of who you are. For example, you have a naturally authoritative voice."

"Don't assume it's natural and therefore others can't do it. It's just a matter of keeping a firm tone and speaking with confidence."

"You make it sound so easy."

"It's not necessarily easy, especially when you're not used to it, but you're not giving advice to people who are going to be going into this seriously, right? It's more for those wanting to role-play to spice up their sex lives. Just advise them to relax and enjoy it."

He picked up the bottle of wine and topped up her glass, then his own. "By the way, how did your practice session go the other day with your friend?"

Dare watched Ashley. He could tell she'd been unhappy when he'd said their sexual relationship would end when he finished his business here in town. Could she really believe they had a future?

He was sure it was just her insecurities kicking in. She was clearly interested in this friend of hers.

She rubbed her hands along her denim-clad thighs, making him too aware of how much he'd like to feel those lovely, long legs around his waist again. With her, naked and moaning, in his arms.

"It went okay." Then she frowned. "It was a bit awkward, actually."

"What happened?"

"I wasn't very sure of myself. He helped, though. He guided me a little by asking what you and I had done together, then suggesting we do that."

He raised an eyebrow. "So you watched a movie?"

She nodded.

"So after you gave him some commands to set it up, did he just kneel by your feet and watch the movie, or did you tell him about being disobedient then have to punish him like I did to you?"

Her cheeks flushed nicely at that.

"Tell me," he said.

Did his sweet Ash actually slap the man's ass? Did she order him to drop his pants? The thought sent heat straight to his groin, and at the same time a surge of jealousy spiked through him. What the hell was that about?

"I just . . . verbally punished him."

She was lying. He knew it. But he wouldn't call her on it, because he could tell something about the situation had upset her.

"So this man and you are good friends?"

"Yes, we're pretty close."

"Do you feel he'd be willing to commit to helping you with this?"

"I think so. Why?"

He smiled. "I was thinking that you might talk him into joining us for a few sessions."

•   •   •

When Dare had suggested Adam join them for some sessions, Ashley had gone into shock. Did he mean for the three of them to . . . Oh, God. But then she realized he just meant to meet Adam and give them some pointers as to how she and Adam could practice together.

And she suspected he wanted to push the two of them together, so he wouldn't feel so bad walking away.

She explained to him that Adam would not be interested.

"You're quiet this morning," Adam said as they ran along the tree-lined path together. He glanced her way. "Is it because of what happened when I came over the other night? Because I'll do whatever I can to make it right between us. I'm really sorry about the kiss."

"No," she said, "it's okay."

But that was a lie. The whole thing, especially his rejection, made her uncomfortable. She had really thought that when he kissed her, they had finally breached the barrier between them and they could move on to a closer, more intimate relationship. One full of possibilities. But he had rejected that.

They were still friends, though, and she wanted that to keep being true.

"Are we still getting together tonight?" she asked. "I still need help with my research."

"Yeah, of course."

She had half expected him to refuse after the awkwardness of last time, but Adam always supported her and it seemed he wouldn't let an unwanted kiss get in the way of that.

God, she desperately wanted to be in a romantic relationship with either one of these phenomenal men, but they
had both rejected her on that front. She was starting to
wonder if there was something wrong with her.

Adam took the bottle of beer Ashley handed him, then
watched her sit down across from him with her glass of
soda. She looked so pretty in her snug jeans and floral top
that accentuated her full breasts, revealing just enough
cleavage to be alluring but not blatantly sexy.

Except she was always sexy to him.

"So how do we start this time?" he asked.

"I'm not really sure. Maybe I could just direct you to
clean the apartment." She smiled. "The carpets could use
vacuuming."

"I think I'd just take the punishment then."

"So that's how it's going to be? If you don't like what
I suggest, then you'll just disobey? How will I learn that
way?"

He laughed. "I suppose once you really have the
hang of it, you'll be able to overcome my willful disobe-
dience."

"Yeah, thanks. I think I need a little more coopera-
tion while I'm learning."

"All right. Why don't we do like last time and repeat
what you did with your mentor."

His smile faded as her cheeks blossomed a deep rose
tone and she glanced away, taking a quick sip of her soda.

Fuck, she'd had sex with Dare. Adam's stomach clenched
at the thought. God damn it, he'd kissed her the last time
they were together, giving him the perfect opportunity

to pursue a relationship with her, but he'd fucking backed off. Now she was fucking Dare.

Dare, of all people!

Jealousy blazed through him.

"Ash, are you getting involved with this guy?"

She curled her legs close to her body. "I don't know." She compressed her lips. "I mean, no, not really."

"You don't sound very sure."

"I don't really want to talk to you about this."

"Why? I thought we were friends."

She glanced at him, their gazes connecting for a second, then she tore hers away. But for that brief moment, he thought he saw a need in her eyes. Could it be that she wanted their relationship to be more than it was, too?

She placed her glass on the table and sat up straight. "You're right. You are my friend and there's no reason we can't talk about this." She looked at him. "I find him attractive. And we . . . uh . . . slept together. But he says it will only last as long as he's in town, which is only another month."

Adam's gut clenched. Even though he'd already figured it out, hearing her admit that she'd had sex with the man had a profound effect on him.

He was relieved that Dare didn't want a long-term relationship with her, but the thought of him touching her, even for a temporary tryst, was sheer torture.

"So break it off, Ash."

"What?"

"Stop seeing him. Continuing will only be harder on you when it ends, and if he doesn't see a future for the two of you, why put yourself through it?"

She stared at him, her face drawn tight with determination. "No, I'm not willing to do that."

Damn it, she was falling for him. He could see it in her eyes.

Fuck, was he going to lose her before he even had her?

He understood the pitfalls of pursuing a relationship with her, but . . . Fuck, the thought of never holding her in his arms or feeling her sweet body pressed to his—never being buried in her velvety depths—made him ache. He wanted to guide her to the blissful ecstasy of complete surrender where she left herself totally vulnerable to him. He wanted to own her, body and soul, and to show her the sweet release only he could give her.

He stood up and walked toward her, then took her hand and pulled her to her feet. Then she was in his arms and his mouth was covering hers. She stiffened at first, clearly in shock at his action, then she relaxed, her soft body melting against him. His tongue nudged against the seam of her mouth and she opened.

The feel of the velvety warmth of her mouth sent his need rocketing. He glided his tongue deep into her and she . . . God, she sucked on it, drawing it deeper.

He pulled her closer, his growing cock squeezed tight between their bodies.

She must have felt it, because she flattened her hands on his chest and pressed. He immediately eased back. But he didn't release her from his embrace.

"I don't understand," she said. "When we kissed last time . . . You already told me you don't want me."

"Don't want you? Fuck, Ash, I've wanted you from the

first moment I laid eyes on you." His lips brushed hers in a light kiss, determined to convince her.

"But you said you were worried about the fact that you're older than me. And it'll be complicated because you're my boss."

He stroked her hair back. "Maybe I've just been an idiot. Maybe none of that matters."

"It doesn't matter to me."

He cupped her head, then drew her face to his and took her lips with passion. When he released them, she was breathless.

She smiled.

"I can't believe it. I've wanted you for such a long time." She stroked his cheek, her hand soft against his whisker-roughened skin. Her big, blue eyes were filled with joy and she leaned closer. Her sweet mouth beckoned and he brushed his lips to hers. She opened, then glided her tongue into his mouth. He sucked it lightly at first, then harder, pulling it deeper. His hands wandered down her back, then he pulled her tight to him as their tongues tangled.

Her breasts heaved against him and his cock swelled thicker.

"God, I want you, sweetheart. I want to drag you into the bedroom and overwhelm your senses until you surrender to me completely."

He could feel her shiver in his arms.

"Oh, yes, Adam. I want that, too."

He couldn't believe this was really happening. He was about to have his dream come true.

He grabbed her hand and led her to the bedroom.

"Wait! What about Dare?"

"What about him?"

She tugged his hand back and he stopped and turned to her.

"Adam, as much as I want this, you've got to understand . . . I'm not willing to walk away from Dare."

His jaw clenched and he coiled his hand in her hair and tugged her head back, exposing her neck. He pressed his lips to her throat and nuzzled, delighted at her gasp of pleasure, then he nipped her skin.

"But you're willing to walk away from me?" His hand stroked down her spine and he pressed it flat to the small of her back and pulled her tightly to him. His hard, swollen cock dug into her belly. "I can leave you a melting puddle on the floor."

She gazed up at him with wide eyes, desire heating the blue depths.

"I believe you."

"So it's settled."

She pressed against his chest, forcing distance between them. "No, it's not. It's only fair for me to be honest with you, Adam. Dare's here for another month and I'm going to keep seeing him as long as I can." She bit her lip as she gazed up at him. "After that, then we could—"

"Are you fucking kidding me? Are you really asking me if I'll wait?"

She didn't answer, but the hope in those wide blue eyes told him that's exactly what she was asking.

He gritted his teeth, staring deep into her eyes as if he could convince her to change her mind by sheer force of will, but it became clear she wasn't going to. Finally, he released her and stepped back.

"I'm sorry, Adam. I don't want to risk losing your friendship, or the chance for us to explore a relationship between us."

He glared at her. "But that's exactly what you're doing."

Ashley knocked on Dare's door. A moment later, he opened it.

"What are you doing here, Ashley? Our session isn't until Friday."

"I know, I . . ." She sucked in a breath. "I had a fight with . . . my friend."

He held the door wide. "Come in."

She scooted into his elegant foyer. He closed the door behind her, then when he turned to her, she stepped into his arms.

"Would you like to stay here tonight?"

She nodded, her head resting against his chest, hearing his heart beating. And hating herself for hoping he'd sweep her into his bed and show her the same passionate loving he had the last time they were together.

She wanted to feel his hard, naked body against her. To be consumed by his overwhelming masculinity.

He led her to his room and ordered her out of her clothes, but when he took her in his arms again, he kissed her with tenderness. When they joined it was a passionate, joyful union, sending her heart soaring.

But when she lay in his arms afterward, his warm body

wrapped around her, she wondered if she'd made a mistake. Not that she wanted to give up Dare. The mere thought sent her cascading to depression. But she'd had an opportunity to start a relationship with Adam, a man she'd been longing for for a long time. A man she believed she could forge a long-term relationship with. And she'd blown him off, insisting she wouldn't give up Dare.

But Dare only wanted her for now. They had no future.

"It doesn't have to be over, you know."

"What?" Her heart thudded in her chest at Dare's words.

"Your friendship with him. From what you've told me, you two are very close, and I don't believe he'll give you up that easily."

"He seemed pretty convincing."

"Just give him time." He nuzzled her ear. "Now go to sleep. Everything will look better in the morning."

Ashley awoke to the sun shining brightly and the smell of bacon wafting around her. Her eyelids popped open and she sat up.

A moment later, the door opened and Dare smiled from the doorway. He was heart-stoppingly gorgeous in just his jeans and bare chest. A broad, sculpted chest that she knew was rock hard, with muscles that rippled when he moved his arms.

A ridiculously hot guy and bacon. Could this morning get any better?

"Come down and have breakfast," he said.

"I need to shower and change first."

"Nonsense. Relax and come join me." He walked to

his closet and pulled out a robe, then tossed it on the bed. "It'll be a bit big, but I like the idea of you wrapped up in my robe."

She picked it up, luxuriating in the feel of the soft silk. She glanced at him, waiting for him to turn away while she pulled on the garment, but he didn't. He just smiled at her. So she pushed back the covers, exposing her nakedness, then stood up and pulled on the robe. Knowing he was watching her sent heat through her and she wanted to entice him to join her in bed again.

But the bacon beckoned, and there was always after breakfast.

She followed him down the stairs, then into the dining room. She sat down and poured herself a coffee from the thermos on the table while he returned to the kitchen. He appeared a moment later with two plates of bacon and scrambled eggs.

She ate a strip of bacon and then took a bite of the eggs. "Mmm. These are delicious."

"I add some herbs to the eggs to make them a bit more exciting."

She couldn't believe Dare could cook. She'd imagined he'd have someone do that for him. Like a maid, or one of his subs. In fact, she was surprised he hadn't ordered her out of bed to make breakfast for him.

A knock sounded at the door.

He continued eating.

"Aren't you going to answer that?" she asked.

"I'm not expecting anyone at this time of the morning, and I see no reason to interrupt a nice breakfast for an impolite stranger."

But the knock sounded again. At the third one, he sighed and pushed himself to his feet. He walked to the door and pulled it open.

"Daddy, it's so good to see you."

Ashley froze at that voice. She pulled the robe tighter around her as she glanced at the door. She wanted to run. To hide. Anything to prevent being seen by the newcomer.

Helen threw herself into Dare's arms and his arms reluctantly slid around her.

"What are you doing here?" he asked.

"Can't I come and visit my dad?"

"I'm not your dad."

Helen fluttered her hand in the air dismissively. "Okay, my stepdad." She glanced toward the dining room. "Oh, I see you have a guest. Anyone I know?"

"Helen, another time would be better."

But Helen dodged past him and marched toward the dining room. As she marched toward Ashley, her expression suddenly switched from determination to one of confusion. Then she clenched her jaw and looked even more solemn. She stopped beside the table and glared at Ashley.

"I thought it was Jessica fucking my stepfather," she muttered loud enough for just Ashley to hear. "But it seems you're the little slut doing him." Her eyes narrowed. "Well, believe me, I'll make sure you pay for this."

Part Two

Ashley's stomach clenched. She hadn't seen Helen in six years, and she had missed her, but now she was confronted by a vindictive, angry woman she barely recognized.

Of course, she could understand Helen being upset at finding Ashley here, in her stepfather's robe, clearly having spent the night. She simply stared into Helen's blazing brown eyes, at a loss for words.

"Helen, what are you doing in town?" Dare asked.

Helen had moved away from Autumn's Ridge years ago, and Ashley had heard that she was living near her mother in Cambria, a town about a hundred miles south.

Helen dragged her gaze from Ashley's, then her sour expression blossomed to one of adoration as she turned to Dare again.

"I heard you were in town on business for a while so I thought I'd come visit. It'll give me a chance to catch up with a few old friends, too." Her sharp gaze flickered to Ashley. "Of course I hadn't expected one of them to be sleeping over."

"Helen . . ."

At Dare's warning tone, she sent him a sugary smile. "You don't mind me coming to visit, do you?"

"Some warning would have been nice."

"Yes, I suppose that would have prevented this awkward situation. So I'll just go get settled in my room."

She grabbed the handle to her suitcase and rolled it across the room, then down the hall.

Dare walked toward the table.

"I'm sorry about that, Ash. She does this kind of thing."

"It's okay. I'll get dressed and head home."

"You don't have to leave."

Ashley stood up. "But it's best if I do. I don't think either one of us wants to suffer the awkwardness of me staying."

She walked to the bedroom and pulled on her clothes. She'd have to rush home to shower and change if she was going to make it to work on time. When she walked back into the living room, thankfully, there was no sign of Helen.

Dare intercepted her at the door and drew her into his arms. He was still in just his jeans and bare chested and the feel of his hot, hard flesh against her set her insides aflame. His lips found hers and the lingering kiss made her want to take his hand and drag him back to the bedroom.

But Helen was just down the hall and that thought was like a bucket of cold water splashing over her.

Reluctantly, she drew her mouth from his. "I've got to go." Then she turned and slipped out the door.

When Ashley got to work, she walked past Adam's office to her desk in the pit, as they called it. An open workspace with half dividers where the staff writers and production staff worked. Adam's door was closed.

She dug her journal from her purse and started up her computer. After opening a new document in her word processor, she began compiling the notes she'd been keeping about her research. She kept an eye on Adam's office door but it was closed all morning. She didn't know what she'd say or do once she saw him, but they had to find a way to get past the tension between them. They were both professionals, so she knew they'd get by, but she wanted more than that.

He was her friend. And he could be so much more. But it seemed that would only happen if she was willing to give up her time with Dare.

Why did things have to be so complicated?

After lunch, she did some online research to incorporate into her article, digging more into the BDSM lifestyle. It was fascinating to discover the levels of control people allowed. There were submissives—subs, for short—who gave up control to their Dominant, the latter often spelled with an uppercase *D,* but some people took it even further. Some people would essentially become a slave to another person, often calling that person *Master.* Surrendering so completely to their Master that they made no decisions of their own, even signing over all their possessions.

She learned more about punishment, too. Flogging, spanking, paddling. How the sub would get excited by the pain. Even come to crave it.

Her cheeks heated as she remembered how it felt to be spanked by Dare. How much it had turned her on.

She closed her browser and tried to focus on organizing

and reviewing what she had pulled together, but it all
reminded her of Dare and his fiery touch. The way his
commanding voice burned through her to kindle a flame
deep inside her that burned hotter than anything she'd
ever known before.

This craving to be dominated—to allow herself to
surrender totally to his will, and her own desires—was
powerful. So powerful she was willing to give up what
she might have with Adam just to have another few weeks
of it with Dare. Because Dare wielded a control over her
that set her free.

"Ashley, come into my office."

Startled, Ashley glanced up to see Adam standing beside her desk. His words were curt, unlike his usual friendly
tone. She stood up and followed him, becoming aware that
the pit was empty. She hadn't realized how late it was—
after six—and most people had left for the day.

She followed him into his office.

"Close the door," he said as he walked to his desk and
leaned back against it.

She closed the door and then approached him uncertainly.

She didn't know what she'd done wrong but his somber expression assured her he wasn't happy with her. Her
throat tightened. She knew he was upset about her turning him down the other night, but it wasn't like Adam to
allow their personal lives to affect them at work. They'd
never really had an argument before, though, and certainly
not one so emotionally charged, so they were definitely
in uncharted territory.

"What's wrong, Adam?"

*   *   *

Everything inside Adam told him this was a mistake, but he pushed aside the uncertainty.

"I didn't want to do this in the office, but you wouldn't return my texts."

"What?" Startled, she grabbed her phone from her jacket and stared at the display. "Oh, I didn't have my charger last night and . . ." She shrugged. "Well, I have to replace my battery. It doesn't hold a charge much these days."

His gut clenched. The only reason she wouldn't have her phone charger was because she hadn't slept at home.

"You spent last night with him."

It killed him that she'd gone straight from him to Dare. After their conversation yesterday . . . Fuck, he'd hoped she'd at least *think* about the situation before going back and screwing Dare.

Her lips compressed, but she didn't say anything.

"Doesn't it bother you at all that he's older than you? And your best friend's stepfather?"

She lowered her gaze, wringing her hands together. "I didn't think so. I mean at first, but . . . he's only ten years older—Helen's mom was kind of a cougar. And we're adults now. It shouldn't matter."

What was going on here? Something had shaken her confidence.

"It shouldn't, but . . . ?"

She just shook her head, but he wasn't in the mood for evasion.

"Talk," he demanded.

She started, her gaze flickering to his. He knew she wasn't used to him talking to her so sharply.

"I . . . uh . . ."

"What happened?" he prompted.

She sighed and wrung her hands even tighter. "You're right. I spent the night with him, then this morning . . . when we were having breakfast . . . Helen showed up."

Helen. Oh, shit. That meant trouble. For Ashley. For Dare.

And for him.

"I take it she wasn't happy finding you there."

Ash shook her head. "Especially not in her stepfather's robe."

His lips compressed. "I imagine she wouldn't like that." He didn't, either.

He drew in a breath. She had to be shaken, and part of him wanted to take care of her, but he couldn't allow that to distract him from his goal.

"Ash, I know you'd probably love for me to offer a shoulder to cry on . . . to be able to talk this out with me . . . because we're friends. But right now I have no interest in helping you patch things up with your lover." He pushed himself forward and closed the distance between them. "Because I don't want you to be with him."

He reached down and grabbed her hand, then drew her to her feet. "I want you. I have for a long time," he said solemnly.

Then he dragged her into his arms and kissed her. She was stiff at first, resisting, but then her body relaxed. Her lips turned soft and yielding under his so he deepened the kiss, gliding his tongue into her mouth. He could feel her body quivering against him.

Then she drew back. "Adam, I—"

He stopped her words with another kiss, driving his tongue deep. He mastered her mouth, thrusting and stroking, then he softened his approach and caressed her back as he suckled her tongue. Her soft body melted against him and her arms slid around him. She clung to him, pulling him closer to her.

"I can be whatever you want," he murmured against her mouth, then nibbled her lips.

When he suckled her lower lip gently, she sighed sweetly.

Then in a sudden movement, he turned her and backed her to the wall, then crushed her against it with his body. She sucked in a breath and stared at him with wide eyes. "So if you like it rough . . . if you want a man to control you . . . believe me, I can do that."

He found her neck and sucked hard on the delicate flesh, feeling her shiver against him. He ground his hips against her, his erection pulsing against her belly as he marked her as his own. God, he wanted to be inside her. When he released her neck, he saw the angry red mark where he'd drawn the blood to the surface.

Let her explain *that* to her lover.

Her hands slid to his shoulders and she pressed against him. He eased back, giving her a little space.

"Adam, please, you know I'm seeing Dare."

He raised an eyebrow. "You aren't *seeing* him. You're screwing him. He's going to walk away in a month." He stroked her hair from her face. "But me, I'm still going to be here." He gave her a predatory smile. "And I'm your boss. If you like being dominated, I can call you into my office any time, order you to strip, and fuck you hard against my desk. Tell me you wouldn't like that," he demanded.

He could tell she would by the hunger flickering in her eyes. And that hunger triggered a need in him so deep, he could barely stop himself from crushing her to the wall and driving into her right here and now.

He pressed his lips to her ear. "Tell me," he insisted.

She stared at him with wide eyes. "I don't know, I . . ." She shook her head. "I've never seen you like this."

He cupped her breast. The softness of it in his hand was almost his undoing. He could barely stop himself from ripping open her blouse and burying his face in her delicious curves.

She arched against him and he could feel her hard nipple through the fabric.

"I want you right now, Ash. And I know you feel the same way."

He captured her mouth, driving his tongue deep as he ground his cock against her again. His swollen, aching member demanded to be freed. To find her hot, slick core and drive deep inside.

"Tell me you want me, too," he insisted.

"Yes. I mean no." She shook her head. "I'm confused. I want you, but I already told you I don't want to end it with Dare. And . . . even though he'll be leaving in a month, I keep hoping . . ." She locked gazes with him. "I'm sorry, I need to be honest with you. I'm going to try and convince him to continue what we've started."

.   .   .

Ashley enjoyed the breeze across her cheek as she sat on the patio of the small bistro sipping her drink. She watched the people walk by on the flower-lined sidewalk as she waited for Jessica to show up.

She couldn't believe what had happened in Adam's office. She stared at the droplets of condensed water gliding down her tall, ice-filled drink.

Oh, God, when he'd pulled her into his arms . . . when he'd kissed her with such passion . . . when his hand had cupped her breast . . . Her heart pounded at the memory. She'd wanted to melt into his arms. To strip off her clothes and let him take her right there.

But it was so confusing. She wanted to be with Adam so much. Knew she could build a happy future with him. But what Dare gave her . . . It was like an obsession. Even if it would only last a month, she wouldn't give it up for anything. Even Adam.

Adam might be willing to take charge, but it wouldn't be the same. There was something about Dare's brand of domination that was like nothing she'd ever imagined. Or was it just Dare himself? Something about the man that she craved?

"Hey, you look deep in thought." Jessica tossed her purse over the back of the chair across from Ashley and sat down, then flagged the waitress. "Tough day?"

The waitress appeared and Jessica ordered a drink.

"An interesting day," Ashley responded to Jessica's question.

"Yeah? What happened?" Jessica plucked her napkin and smoothed it on her lap.

"Adam called me into his office and . . . well, he made it clear he wants to start something with me."

"About time. You two have been skirting your attraction for far too long."

Ashley sipped her drink, the ice cubes tinkling against each other.

"But I'm seeing Dare."

Jessica shrugged. "Yeah, but that's just screwing around. It's not serious."

Ashley leaned forward. "But it's amazing. I don't want to give up what I have with Dare."

Jessica shrugged. "Okay, well, maybe Adam will be willing to wait until it's over with Dare. It's just a month."

Ashley raised an eyebrow. "You don't really believe that, do you?" She didn't mention that she'd already suggested it and he hadn't been impressed with the idea.

Jessica rested her chin on her hand. "No, not really. It's too bad, though."

Ashley nodded. "But you know, I've been thinking. And . . . well . . . what if it doesn't have to end in a month with Dare?"

Jessica's eyes sparked with interest. "Did Dare say something?"

Ashley frowned. "No, but . . . I don't want this to slip away. When I'm with him . . . I just . . . I want to surrender to him completely. To be *his*." She shook her head. "I don't want it to end."

Jessica covered Ashley's hand with hers. "Oh, Ash. Are you falling for him?"

"I don't know. We don't know each other well enough yet to really know but . . . I don't want to lose how I feel around him. It may just be intense sexual need . . ." Her face flushed as a woman walking past the table glanced at her and she realized she'd been talking a little too loudly. She lowered her voice and leaned in closer to Jess. "But whatever it is, I don't want it to end. And . . . if I do fall for him . . . I think we could make it work. Despite the age difference. Despite everything."

Now Jess frowned. "Yeah, I'm sure you could, but it won't be easy."

"You mean because of Adam?" Her heart ached. She knew deep inside that she and Adam could have a chance at happiness together. They were so well suited to each other and now that they'd taken the first step past the barriers that had stopped them from proceeding in the past, she believed deep in her heart that if they began seeing each other, they could make it work.

If it didn't work out with Dare . . . There was no reason to believe he'd want to continue with her after this month—long-distance relationships hardly ever worked—but if she made it clear to him that she wanted a future with him . . .

But that wasn't fair to Adam. And Dare wouldn't want her directing how their relationship went. *He* was the one in charge.

"Adam is part of it," Jess said, "but, I mean, there are other complications."

"Like what?"

"Okay, well, I had lunch with Helen today."

"Really? But she only got into town this morning," Ashley said. "I was going to tell you that—"

"She told me she walked in on you and Dare."

Ashley sat up straighter, pulling her shoulders back. "It's not like she walked in on us in the bedroom. I was at the dining room table."

"In Dare's robe. I know."

Some of the old feelings of resentment arose as she remembered when Jess had moved to town and she and Helen had become close, leaving Ash feeling like an out-sider.

"So you think I should back off on Dare because of Helen?"

"No, I'm not saying that. I just wanted to make you aware that Helen is bound and bent to cause you prob-lems. She spent most of lunch trying to convince me you're a conniving gold digger who's after her precious stepdaddy for his money."

At Ashley's wounded expression, Jess squeezed her hand.

"Hey, you know I don't believe that, and I'm not just spreading gossip. I want to warn you that she means trou-ble and there's no reasoning with her."

"She's trying to drive a wedge between us," Ashley said.

"She doesn't realize how close you and I still are. I didn't let her know that, hoping she'd talk more freely. It seems clear she's spreading this nonsense to anyone who'll listen."

"I get that she might not be happy with me seeing her stepfather, but . . ." Ashley shook her head. "In high school, the three of us were so close. After my mom died, you two were all I had. I just don't understand what happened."

Jessica shook her head. "I don't know. But whatever

happened after graduation that caused her to drop out of college before she even started . . . giving up that great scholarship she had for NYU . . . It really messed her up."

"You know, I won't let her manipulate me into giving up Dare. Let her do her damnedest. I don't scare off that easily."

"So you're going to give up on Adam?"

Ashley pursed her lips. "I really care about Adam. Before Dare came along, I would have jumped at the chance to be with him."

"If you had to choose one?"

"I know the sensible choice is Adam. We have so much in common. And . . . well, after our conversation in his office . . ."

"Ha, conversation. I can see from the flush on your cheeks that it was more than that." Jessica grinned. "What happened?"

"He played the dominating boss and . . ." Ashley's cheeks flushed. "I'm not going to lie. It was hot."

"Ah, man. I'd trade places with you in a minute, despite all the drama. If only you didn't have to choose between them."

Dare watched Helen walk across the living room then sink onto the couch across from him. She'd made them both a nice dinner and had insisted on cleaning up on her own.

"How long are you planning on being in town?" Dare asked Helen.

"I don't know. Three or four weeks maybe. It's not set in stone. How long will you be here?"

"I go back to New York at the end of the month.

How's your job going?" He wondered how she could just take several weeks off work.

"Oh, well, I'm between jobs right now. But no worries. I have some money saved up."

He held back the urge to offer financial aid. She might be difficult in a lot of ways, but she never asked for money. But there was this protectiveness he'd always felt for her. She'd been a good kid when he and her mom had been married, but she'd taken the divorce really hard. He'd brought the only stability she'd ever known to her life.

He had no illusions about her. She could be trouble. For herself and for others. But he knew she genuinely cared for him, and wanted to keep their stepfather-stepdaughter relationship alive. In fact, he sometimes wondered if she wanted more than that. The way she hugged him when she saw him . . . the way she kissed him whenever she got the chance . . . He used to put it down to her just wanting a dad, but she lingered too long. Was too affectionate.

He would love to give her the love and affection she craved, but only as a stepfather. But he couldn't do that without her reading too much into it.

Helen definitely had problems. And he wanted to be there for her. But he had to walk a fine line.

But a stern, distant father figure—that he could handle.

"Have you sent out résumés? Are you networking?"

She laughed. "You insist you're not my stepdad, but you like to act like one."

"Helen, you know I'm concerned about you, and I care what happens to you."

She slung her arm behind her head and rested against it. "I'll be fine. Don't worry about me."

"Good." He stood up. "I've got some contracts to go over so I'll see you tomorrow."

He spent the next few hours in his office going over paperwork in preparation for a meeting he had the next day. When he left the den, the lights in the rest of the house were turned off and Helen's door was closed. He sighed a breath of relief and retired to his bedroom. Once he climbed into bed, he lay in the darkness, hoping for sleep, but thoughts of Ashley percolated through his brain.

She had clearly been freaked out this morning when Helen had arrived, and he could hardly blame her. He and Ashley had both been able to ignore their history and difference in ages, until Ashley had come face-to-face with her old friend—his stepdaughter—putting everything in clear perspective for her.

He wouldn't be surprised if she didn't show up on Friday.

But he wanted her to. He'd find a way to get rid of Helen for the night—maybe even the whole weekend—so he could revel in the joy of being with his delightfully submissive Ashley.

He only had a few more weeks here and he intended to enjoy every hour he could with her.

Dare awoke to the quiet thump of his bedroom door closing. He glanced across the room and saw the silhouette of a woman in the moonlight.

"Ashley?"

She walked toward the bed, her long flowing robe hugging her slender body.

"No, Daddy, it's me."

He sat up. "Helen? What's wrong? Did you have a bad dream?"

"No. In fact, I had a delightful dream." She stood a few feet from his bed.

Alarm bells sounded in his head as he saw her fingers glide to the tie around her waist.

"I dreamed about you and me," she said in a sultry voice.

Damn it, she was untying her robe. He leaped from the bed as her tie dropped and the front of the robe slipped open.

"God damn it, Helen." He tugged the robe closed, having only caught sight of a sliver of naked skin, then he grabbed the sash and tied it snuggly at her waist.

"But, Daddy . . ." she murmured, her eyes wide and filled with a disturbing heat.

"Don't call me that."

She ran her hand up his chest, then over his shoulder and she leaned in close. "Then I'll call you Dare. Which is so much better, anyway, because I think it's time for our relationship to move in a new direction."

"Helen, don't even—"

She wrapped her arms around his neck and gazed at him with longing. "But I've wanted you for so long. And I know you want me, too."

He grabbed her wrists and dragged her arms from around him.

"Helen, you know I don't feel that way about you."

"Do I? Then why are you fucking that slut who is my age? I'm sure it's because you really want *me*."

"Don't talk about Ashley that way."

He should deny her claim that he wanted her—which he didn't, sexually. She used to be his stepdaughter, for God's sake, but how did he put that into words that didn't make her feel unwanted as a human being? She'd been abandoned by her own father, and two other stepfathers. Even her mother didn't show her the love she needed. Didn't make her feel like she belonged anywhere. Dare didn't want to hurt her more than she had been already, but he walked a fine line.

She pouted and rested her hand on his chest. "I'm sorry, I just want you so much. Mom was an idiot to walk out on you. I'd never, ever do that."

Her hand glided upward and he flattened his on top of it and drew it away.

"You don't want me, you just think you do."

Before he knew what she was doing, she grabbed her robe and pulled it open, exposing her naked breasts.

Fuck. He pulled it closed again, grasped her shoulders and spun her around, then marched her to the door.

"This is completely inappropriate, Helen." He guided her down the hall to her door, then opened it. "If you try a stunt like this again, you won't be welcome here."

He closed the door behind her, then strode back to his room. This time he locked the door.

Ashley dropped onto the couch and slumped down. She'd tried to arrange a movie with Jessica this evening, but Jess had a date with Eric, a guy from work whom she'd had a crush on for a while.

Ashley sighed. She just wanted something to keep her mind off Dare. She should be over there right now.

Helen coming to town had thrown everything off. With her staying with Dare, Ashley had no idea when she'd see him again, or even if she would before he returned to New York. He wasn't the kind of man to let things just drop between them, though, so she had to trust that she'd hear from him when the time was right.

Her cell phone chimed, indicating a text. She picked it up and glanced at the display.

You're late.

She stared at the message from Dare, her heart lurching.

With Helen there, I thought tonight was canceled, she typed.

Get your ass over here, he replied. *I expect you here within 20 mins.*

She jumped to her feet and ran into the bathroom to refresh her makeup, then she grabbed a sexy bra and panty set from her drawer—sheer black with lacy flowers edging the cups and the skimpy front of the panties. Then she threw on a slinky, formfitting dress in a deep blue print. She was out the front door in record time, her heart pounding in her chest.

She was going to see Dare tonight.

She couldn't stop grinning as she drove to his house, arriving exactly twenty-two minutes after his text. She rang the doorbell.

He opened the door, his face stern. "I said twenty minutes."

"I did my best, but there was traffic," she said as she followed him inside.

"That sounds like an excuse."

She dropped her gaze. "No, sir. I'm sorry I'm late, Mr. Gallagher."

She followed him through the house to *the* door. The room where her deepest fantasies were brought to life.

When he closed the door behind them, she turned to him.

"Where's Helen?" she asked.

"Don't worry about her. She's staying with a friend for the weekend."

She didn't ask if that was because Dare had sent her away or if it was Helen's choice. It didn't matter. All that mattered was that Ashley was here now.

As he stepped closer, her whole body went into alert. Her nerve endings tingling, anticipating his touch. Her insides swirling with need.

He stroked her cheek, his touch like a whisper of electricity grazing her skin. Warmth glowed in his dark blue eyes, and she stared into those depths, noticing the little golden flecks that looked like starlight across a midnight sky.

His lips lowered to hers and brushed lightly, then lingered for scant seconds. Enough to drive her need to dizzying heights, but not enough to satisfy her craving.

"You know I have to punish you."

"Yes, sir."

The eagerness in her eyes caused Dare's pulse to quicken. God, she was delightful.

"First, I want you to change."

"But . . . I thought—"

"What you're wearing is very sexy." And it was. The dress accentuated all her curves, and the short skirt and high heels showed off her long, shapely legs. He didn't

want to discourage her from choices like this one, but he
still wanted her to wear the costume he'd been fantasizing about seeing her in.

He walked to the cupboard and pulled out the box
he'd hidden in there earlier today and handed it to her.
She set it down on the nearest bench and pulled off the lid.
She gazed inside, then picked up the short, blue plaid skirt
and the virginal white blouse.

She grinned at him. "A schoolgirl uniform? Really?
A little cliché, don't you think?" she teased.

He chuckled. "Would you rather the sexy nun costume?"

"Um, no, I'll stick with this." She placed her hand on
his chest. The feel of it set his heart beating faster. "Unless
you're going to put on a sexy priest outfit. Or would you
be a naughty schoolboy and I'd be punishing you?"

"No and no. And I'm not really giving you a choice."

At the subtle hint to drop back into their role as Dom
and sub, she drew her hand away and picked up the blouse.

"Yes, sir."

"I'll give you ten minutes to change." He turned and
left the room, knowing he'd barely be able to wait that
long.

Ashley reached behind her and unzipped the dress, then
let it fall to the floor. She pulled on the blouse and but-
toned it, leaving the top few open, enough to show the lacy
edges of the cups of her bra . . . and quite a bit of cleavage.
Also, the black bra showed through the white fabric like
a dark, sexy shadow. When she pulled on the skirt, she
wished that she'd worn a garter belt, but when she gazed

at herself in the full-length mirror on one wall she realized this looked better. More innocent.

She wondered if she should slip off her panties. The skirt was so short that if she bent over, he'd see everything. But she decided to leave them on.

He strode back into the room just as she was picking up her dress from the ground. She turned around to see that he'd been admiring her backside.

She quickly folded the dress and dropped it in the box that had held the costume.

"Very nice," he said, his gaze roaming her body. "Turn around."

She turned slowly in front of him, feeling her body heat at his close scrutiny.

"Now it's time for your punishment." He walked across the room and sat down on a leather couch. "Come over here."

She walked across the room and stood before him. The pleated plaid skirt was very short and the top of her black bra peeked out from the plunging neckline of the blouse. She felt like a naughty schoolgirl facing her sexy schoolmaster's smoldering gaze.

"First, you were going to skip our session today," he said, his expression stern. "Then when I summoned you here, you were late and you know I'm very strict about that."

"Yes, Mr. Gallagher. I'm sorry, sir."

Heat simmered through her as she thought about his big hand connecting with her ass.

"Sorry isn't good enough. Bend over my knee," he instructed.

She stepped forward and knelt on the leather couch beside him, then bent over him until her stomach rested on his lap, her ass hiked in the air. His hand rested on her thigh, about halfway up and she trembled in anticipation. His fingers curled as his hand glided upward, his finger-tips grazing along her inner thigh. Her breath caught as he approached her panties, thinking he would brush against her dampening crotch, but instead his hand moved toward her ass.

He drew back the fabric of her skirt. Since she was wearing a thong, her ass was basically naked and his big, warm hand cupped her round cheek. He stroked in a cir-cle, sending need spiraling through her. When his hand lifted from her ass, her breath held as she waited for it to whip back down and connect with her bare bottom.

Smack. The sound reverberated through the room as ripples of heat washed through her. Then another quick slap across her other cheek almost made her gasp.

"Do you like that?"

"Oh, yes, sir."

"That's why I won't be giving you any more. This is supposed to be a punishment."

"But, sir—"

"Silence. Now I'll be punishing you for arguing, too. Kneel in front of me."

"Yes, Mr. Gallagher."

She slid off his lap and knelt on the floor facing him. The stiff fabric of the short, pleated skirt still curled up-ward, revealing her naked ass. She could tell he was staring at it in the mirror on the wall behind her.

"You are a selfish little girl and need to learn how to

respect the needs of others." He took her hand and rested it on the front of his pants.

She drew in a breath at the feel of how hard and thick his erection was under the cloth.

"And, as you can tell, I have needs right now." He raised an eyebrow. "What are you going to do about it?"

She stared at the huge bulge under her hand and licked her suddenly dry lips. "I'm going to meet your needs, sir."

"And how are you going to do that?"

"I'm going to unzip your pants and wrap my hand around you. Then I'm going to take it in my mouth."

He nodded. "Very good."

She pulled down his zipper and slid her hand inside his pants. As soon as her fingers wrapped around his hot, smooth flesh, her insides melted and she felt the slickness between her legs. She drew him out and admired his thick, long erection.

"Oh, sir, it's beautiful." She stroked the length of it, the kid-leather soft skin gliding against her palm and fingers. She could see the need burning in his eyes.

She leaned forward and pressed her lips to his tip. Immediately, he glided his fingers through her hair.

"Take it in your mouth," he said, his voice tight.

She opened and he drew her head down, until the entire crown was in her mouth. She swirled her tongue over him then sucked. He pressed her further down his shaft . . . and further. She had to relax and open to let him glide down her throat. Then he drew her back, his fingers tangled in her hair so she had to follow.

He pressed her forward and back, setting a rhythm. A few slow strokes, then several fast, then slow again. He was so hard and thick her throat ached with the effort of keeping it open and as relaxed as she could. Then he released her hair.

"Keep going."

She continued the rhythm, her hand firmly wrapped around his root. Her other hand slid to his balls and she caressed them.

"Oh, fuck."

He jerked into her and hot, salty liquid squirted into her throat. Filling her mouth. She kept bobbing on him as he groaned. When he slumped back, she sucked a little more, then drew back, relinquishing his spent cock from her mouth. She licked the semi-erect shaft, lapping at the smooth skin until every drop was gone. Then she licked some that had dribbled down his testicles. When she was done, she lifted her head.

"Look what you've done." His voice was steely and his eyes glinted. "For what I intend to do to you, I need my cock hard and ready."

He stood up, pulling her to her feet, too. He marched her across the room and directed her to sit on a wooden bench along the wall.

"Put your feet up on the bench on either side of you."

She wasn't quite sure what he wanted, but he grabbed one ankle and lifted it, bending her knee, then set her foot on the wooden surface beside her ass, then did the same with the other. The result left her legs spread wide open to him. His gaze fell on her sheer panties that did nothing to hide her intimate flesh.

His hot gaze bored through her, as if he were gliding

a finger inside her. Finally, she couldn't stop herself from squirming.

His gaze rose to her face, taking in her heated cheeks.

"The way you're dressed. You look like a slut."

He ran his finger along the open neckline of her blouse, tugging slightly to give him a better view of the black bra beneath.

"This isn't exactly part of the school uniform."

She pouted. "I thought it looked pretty, sir."

"You look like a whore." He frowned. "I'm only telling you this for your own good. You could get into a lot of trouble dressed like this."

He unfastened a button on her blouse, and another, then pulled it open to reveal her bra.

"This undergarment is practically transparent," he said. "Your nipples are totally visible."

He ran his thumb over one swollen nub and a shocking jolt of sensation stabbed through her, straight to her core.

"You like it when I touch you there."

"Oh, yes, I do, sir."

He frowned. "You are a very dirty girl. You definitely shouldn't be wearing something like this." He pressed on the front clasp and the bra popped open. He pushed the cups aside, his heated gaze intense on her naked breasts. Her nipples ached with need.

He ran his hand over her breast, then squeezed her nipple between his fingers. It was a painful pleasure and she cried out.

"Did I hurt you?" he asked.

"It's okay, sir." She longed for him to pinch the other one, too.

"But that's not okay. Let me make it feel better."

He knelt in front of her, then leaned forward and kissed her nipple. Then his mouth wrapped around it and his tongue nudged against it. When he suckled, she moaned, then her fingers raked through his hair as she held him close to her bosom. His fingers found her other nipple and he squeezed that one sharply as he continued to suck the first.

"Oh, Mr. Gallagher," she cried.

His mouth shifted and he suckled her stinging nub.

Then she moaned as he drew his mouth away. His gaze fell to her crotch.

"Do you know what boys will do if they see these panties? And with such a short skirt, they're bound to see them."

She shook her head. "No, sir. What will they do?"

He leaned in close, his intense masculine presence sending ripples of awareness through her. "They'll want to touch you. Down there. You wouldn't want that, would you?"

She widened her eyes. "Oh, no, sir." Then she wrapped her hand around his and guided it to her thigh, and murmured softly, "I only want you to touch me there." Then she pressed his fingers to her folds, feeling her own wetness against her fingertips as they briefly brushed her panties.

She thought for a moment he was going to scold her, but then his eyes glittered and a slow smile spread across his face.

"Really?" Then his fingers brushed her sensitive flesh and she moaned.

He hooked his finger around the crotch of her panties and pulled it aside. Then he dragged his gaze from her and leaned forward, staring at her revealed petals of flesh.

"Your pussy is very pretty," he murmured.

His finger brushed over her folds. Then it thrust inside her and she gasped.

"You like that?"

His finger was deep inside her, swirling inside her channel.

"Yes, sir." In fact, the sensations were intoxicating.

But now would he deny her this and find another punishment for her?

He moved his finger inside her, thrusting in and out, driving her desire higher and higher.

Then he withdrew and grabbed her hips, dragging her butt forward, causing her back to curve. His fingers glided along her slick folds. When they glided back, then pressed against her tight back opening, she drew in a breath. One slick finger slid inside her and he twirled it back and forth. A moment later, he gently pushed in another finger, stretching her tight anal opening.

Her eyelids had fallen closed, so she jumped when she felt his mouth brush against her slit. She watched his head move as he licked her. When his mouth found her clit and he began to suck, she cried out. His finger moved in her ass, and the combined sensations took her breath away.

"Oh, sir." Her head fell back against the wall. "Oh, that feels so good."

He lifted his head and smiled, his lips glistening from

her slickness. Then he stood up. His cock, jutting from his pants, was rock hard and pulsing.

"And it's going to feel even better in a moment. I'm going to push my big cock right up your ass."

She quivered at the thought, her legs trembling.

"Daddy?"

At the sound of Helen's voice, Ashley grabbed her blouse and tugged it closed, then sat up, pulling her skirt down. She could see Dare grit his teeth as he pushed his distended cock back into his pants—with some effort—then zipped up.

Ashley could see Helen walking toward them. Dare's back was still to her and his body mostly hid Ashley so she was pretty sure Helen hadn't seen anything too embarrassing.

"What the hell are you doing here, Helen?" he demanded through gritted teeth.

"I didn't know where you were, and I needed to find you." Helen's speech seemed a little slurred.

"Get out right now," Dare commanded.

"No, I won't." Helen's gaze locked on Ashley and scrutinized her costume. "Why are you here with *her*? You're fucking her, aren't you?"

"Helen, this is none of your business."

"But, Daddy—"

"Don't call me that." The anger in his gritty tone was one Ashley would be sure to heed, but Helen seemed nonplussed.

Helen threw herself down on the bench beside Ashley and glared at him. "I could wear a slutty schoolgirl uniform like this. Why won't you fuck me like you do this gold-digging whore?"

At Helen's words, shock vaulted through Ashley.

"Fuck. You're drunk, Helen."

Ashley jumped as Helen's hand fell on Ashley's breast and she squeezed. Ashley tried to pull away, but Helen wrapped her arm around Ashley's waist and held her close to her side. She was surprisingly strong.

"Would you like it if I made out with her?" Helen asked. "I know how that turns men on. If I did that, Daddy, *then* would you fuck me?"

Suddenly, Helen's mouth was on hers and Ashley gasped, trying to free herself from the soft feminine lips and the tongue that thrust inside her mouth. The taste of alcohol was overwhelming.

Then the soft body pulled away and Ashley realized Dare had grabbed Helen's arm and pulled her to her feet. He marched her across the room and out the door.

Ashley sat on the hard bench, sucking in air. That was so embarrassing. And disturbing.

Clearly, Helen had been coming on to Dare. Oh, God, she didn't even want to think about it.

But now here she sat, still hot and needy for Dare. She started to button her blouse, but then the door opened and Dare strode toward her.

"Don't touch those buttons," he demanded.

When he reached her, he tugged her to her feet and into his arms. His mouth captured hers and his tongue plunged inside her mouth. But as frantically sexy as this was, her gaze shifted to the door. She pulled away.

"But Helen—"

"I locked her in her room. She won't disturb us again."

"Locked her in? But . . ."

"Don't worry about it. I don't want her wandering off in her state. She needs to sleep it off."

He pulled her tighter to his body, his thick shaft rock hard against her belly. "And we need to finish what we started. I am so fucking ready for you. What we did earlier has me so hot there's no way I could wait to be inside you."

He cupped her breast, then stroked. Heat burst through her as he pinched her nipple until it was swollen with need.

God, she wanted him inside her. She found his pants and fumbled with the zipper until she could reach inside and grasp his throbbing shaft.

He consumed her mouth as she stroked his erection.

He backed her up against the wall. "Open your legs," he demanded.

She obeyed and was rewarded by the feel of his hot flesh gliding over her slick folds.

"I'm going to fucking take you against this wall," he murmured fiercely against her ear, then nipped her earlobe. Sharp pangs spiked through her as his teeth abraded her tender skin.

Then his pelvis surged forward. His thick column drove into her, stretching her canal wide. She tightened her arms around him, clutching him close while they both panted for air, his big cock buried deep inside her.

He moved and the feel of him shifting inside her made her moan.

"Oh, Dare, please fuck me."

"God damn." He pulled out, then drove forward again.

Her insides ached as his enormous cock thrust into her again and again. She quivered and the intense pleasure almost made her weep.

Still he drove in and out. Stroking her passage. His cock thrusting purposefully. Making her sing with pleasure. Her voice grew higher and higher as the pleasure pulsed inside her, until it was a high squeal of delight.

"Say my name again." The need in his voice matched her own.

"Dare. Oh, Dare, make me come."

"Yes . . . baby . . . Come . . . for . . . me." He uttered the words between thrusts.

Pleasure swelled and her senses flared to a tingling mass of need.

"Yes, I . . . Ohhh," she moaned as joy swept through her. "I'm coming." The last word trailed to a reedy wail.

Then ecstasy burst through her, carrying her on the wings of blissful delight. Soaring into the unknown.

His body pulsed against her, his cock swelling, then he groaned as it erupted inside her in a spasm of joyful release. He buried his face in her hair as his body shuddered in ecstasy.

They clung to each other, both shivering in the aftermath.

Finally, he drew back and his lips found hers. His kiss, tender and passionate, reached right into her heart and stroked it.

She meant something to him. After that, she knew she must.

He drew back, but instead of the smile she anticipated, his face was drawn tight in concern.

He cupped her cheeks and kissed her again.

"I'm sorry but you'll have to go now."

Ashley sat in her car in Dare's driveway, now back in the clothes she'd worn to Dare's this evening, a bit in shock. He hadn't even watched from the window to see if she got into her car okay.

She knew he was concerned about Helen, but she felt rejected.

Ashley pushed the key into the ignition and started the car.

She had no idea what to think about Helen's behavior. What she had done tonight was embarrassing and disturbing. Ashley didn't even want to think about it, but she couldn't get the thought of Helen begging her ex-stepfather to fuck her out of her mind.

God, the woman was so screwed up. Woman? Actually, she had acted more like a spoiled teenager. A teenager who would do anything for attention.

Dare had his work cut out for him straightening her out. Ashley wondered if she should go back in there. Maybe she could help.

Should she really leave Dare alone with Helen when she might throw herself at him?

No, she was being silly. Dare would never succumb to Helen's strange and disturbing bid for attention. He was strong and always in control.

But now Ashley felt rejected. If it hadn't been for

Helen, Ash would probably be curled up in Dare's arms in bed. But he'd chosen Helen over her.

She knew she shouldn't let that bother her, but she couldn't help it.

Dare raked his hand through his hair as he paced the living room, phone to his ear. The answering machine picked up on the other end, so he disconnected then dialed again. Sometimes Ann would pick up after several tries.

The third time dialing, he heard a click on the other end.

"Hello?" Ann's voice sounded short.

"It's Dare."

"What do you want?" she asked. Same Ann. Short and to the point.

"You should come and get Helen."

"She's with you in New York?"

He strode to the armchair and sat down.

"No, Autumn's Ridge. I'm here on business for a few weeks. You didn't know where she was?"

"Why should I? I don't keep track of her."

"Well, she's having a problem. I think she could use her mother."

"Is she sick or injured?"

He glanced down the hall toward the bedrooms, knowing Helen was in the guest room, probably passed out.

"No, but she got stinking drunk."

"Of course she did." At her tone, he imagined Ann rolling her eyes. "If she made a mess of things, then it's up to her to clean it up. I'm not babysitting her."

Good old Ann. She didn't care about her daughter, or the fact that Helen might have caused problems for him. Ann lived in her own selfish little world, looking out for number one and no one else. No wonder Helen was so screwed up.

No wonder Helen felt so unwanted.

"That's pretty callous, Ann."

"Look, she's an adult now, which means she's not my problem anymore. She has to learn to take care of herself." Then she hung up the phone.

Dare jabbed the End button, then dropped the phone in its dock.

Fuck! The way Helen was acting, he should toss her out on her ass, but he couldn't do that to her. He knew that her behavior was a cry for help and he couldn't just abandon her, no matter how much she might mess up his life.

And his relationship with Ashley.

God, he wished Ashley hadn't seen that. Helen calling her names, then coming on to him like that. And touching Ash inappropriately. It must have been horrendous for her.

And after he'd marched Helen to her room, he'd gone back and continued the fuck session with Ash, still so turned on by what they'd been doing he couldn't help himself.

After the stunningly erotic sex, the blood flow had returned to his brain, and he'd begun to worry about Helen again.

The expression on Ashley's face when he'd rushed her out of the house still haunted him. She'd looked so rejected.

He gritted his teeth, knowing he couldn't think about that now. He'd find a way to make it up to her. Somehow. But right now, he had to make some arrangements for Helen. He picked up the phone. He wouldn't abandon Helen like her mother seemed perfectly content to do.

As the phone rang on the other end, his thoughts turned back to Ashley. He loved being with her and regretted that his time with her would be interrupted by Helen's issues. He knew Ash probably wouldn't be open to a long-term relationship with him. He wouldn't mistake her excitement at being dominated with real feelings for him, especially given their age difference and the fact he'd been her friend's stepfather, but he had looked forward to a solid few weeks of enjoying her ongoing discovery of her submissive side.

Now he realized that, as much as they both enjoyed him mentoring her, she'd probably be better off if they ended it now.

Ashley's phone chimed, signaling a text. She finished the e-mail she was working on, then picked it up, hoping it was from Dare.

Just finished with a client near your office. Want to grab a coffee?

It was from Jessica.

Yeah, sure, Ashley responded.

She'd be happy to get out of the office for a little while. Since what happened between her and Adam the other evening, he'd been keeping his distance, not wanting to make her uncomfortable in the workplace, but she was still on edge.

She grabbed her purse and headed to the Starbucks on the corner where Jess said she'd be waiting for her.

"Hey, there you are," Jess said as Ashley dropped her purse on a spare chair and sat down.

There were already two coffees sitting on the table.

"My treat," Jess said. "It's that new latte you tried the other day and liked so much."

Ashley smiled and took a sip. "Thanks. So you're pretty chipper this morning."

"Yeah, well, things are going pretty well with Eric."

"That's great," Ashley said, glad her friend's love life was going smoother than her own right now. "So are you going to kiss and tell?"

Jess laughed. "Well, there's not much to tell except that we did kiss. It was a first date." She grinned. "But talk to me after our second date and we'll see."

Ashley smiled. "He asked you out again. That's great."

Jessica had been so nervous about how things would go, because she really liked this guy. Ashley was happy that things seemed to be heading off to a good start.

"It may not be as exciting as you seeing a billionaire Dom who makes you surrender to his every sexual whim"—she grinned—"but, you never know."

"Well, not everyone's as lucky as me." Ashley had meant it to sound lighthearted, but her words came across with an edge that caught Jessica's attention and she frowned.

"Hey, what's up?"

Ashley shook her head. "Oh, no, nothing." She didn't want to bring Jessica down from her euphoria of starting a relationship with someone special.

"Don't do that. I can see it in your eyes. What happened?"

Ashley frowned, her hand tightening around the warm coffee cup in front of her.

"When I was at Dare's last time, it got a bit . . . tense. Not between him and me, but . . ." She shook her head, her cheeks heating. "Helen showed up."

"Showed up? So she caught you at Dare's house again?"

Ashley sucked in a breath. "She caught Dare and I . . . *together*." She hadn't intended to tell Jessica that. It had just slipped out. But Jess was her best friend and she knew if anyone could make her feel less crappy about the situation—less mortified—it would be her.

"Oh, God, that's . . . awkward."

Ashley nodded. "You have no idea."

"What did she do?"

Okay, there was no way Ashley was going to give her details.

"Well, she didn't just leave. She was just . . ." A shiver raced through Ashley as she remembered. "I don't know. I don't really want to talk about that, but . . ." She stared at her coffee cup. "I think she'd been drinking."

Jessica nodded. "Did you know she used to drink in high school?"

Ashley gazed at her friend. "Well, sure, we all used to sneak one sometimes."

"No, I mean, she used to drink in school. She carried a flask around in her purse."

"Really?"

"Yeah, I caught her one day and she made me swear to secrecy. Her parents—well, her mom and Dare—were going through some rough times, leading up to the divorce. They didn't tell her they were getting divorced until after graduation, but I suspect Helen knew it was coming, or was afraid it was, anyway."

"And you didn't tell me?" Ashley felt a little hurt.

Jess shrugged. "I wouldn't have told her if you had told me something sensitive and swore me to silence."

Ashley nodded. "Of course. Sorry."

"So right now life is kind of sucky for you. You've got an awkward situation with Dare, since Helen is in the picture, and it's got to be tense with you and Adam. How's that going?"

"We have sort of an unspoken agreement to give each other space in the office and he suggested that we suspend our usual running and movie night for now."

"I can't imagine that's going to last long. I'm sure he's going to make another move soon. To convince you to change your mind and start seeing him."

Ashley shook her head. "I just wish everything wasn't so complicated."

Jessica smiled. "Yeah, well, that's what happens when you get involved with these older, dominant types," she teased. "They turn your world upside down." She took Ashley's hand and squeezed. "You know, I think you should just have sex with both of them. Preferably at the same time."

"Jess, you're terrible."

"Why? Because I suggest you live out every woman's fantasy? Don't tell me you haven't thought about it."

Ashley sat at her desk, staring at the computer screen.

Being with both Dare and Adam. She *hadn't* thought

about it until Jessica mentioned it, but now she couldn't *stop* thinking about it.

What would it be like to have one sucking her breasts, his hand stroking her inner thigh, while the other nuzzled her neck from behind? Being sandwiched between their two big, muscular bodies while their hard cocks glided into her, filling her with wild pleasure.

Her phone rang, startling her from her revery. Cheeks heating, she picked it up.

"Ashley? It's Dare."

Her back stiffened and her cheeks grew hotter.

"Oh, yes. Hi."

"I was hoping you could meet me for dinner. Tonight. Around six?"

That was less than an hour from now.

"I'll need a little more time than that. I have to go home and change first."

"That's not necessary."

"But I'm just in jeans." And she'd like to put something sexy on for him.

"It's okay. We'll go somewhere casual. I can pick you up from the office if you'd like."

"Sure." She glanced at the clock on her computer. "How about forty minutes?"

She finished up a bit of paperwork, then grabbed her purse. When she walked out the front of her office building, Dare was waiting there in his sporty silver car. He got out and opened the door for her, helping her into the low seat then, a moment later, he put the car into gear and pulled into the city traffic.

He took her to a roadhouse on the edge of the city,

not too far from her apartment. It was very rustic, with solid wood tables that had been polished to a glossy shine and waiters dressed in black pants and plaid shirts. Dare asked for a quiet booth and the hostess led them to a corner of the restaurant.

"I wanted to apologize about what happened the other night with Helen," he said.

She bit her lip. "Thank you. That was pretty awkward. Is Helen okay?"

His gaze jerked to hers. "Why do you ask that?"

"Well, she was pretty drunk."

His lips compressed. "Yes, her judgment was impaired, but that's no excuse for her wildly inappropriate behavior. Again, I'm sorry."

Ashley nodded. "Thank you." There didn't seem to be anything else to say. Though she wondered if he'd send Helen away now. Boot her out on her ass after what she did.

If he did, then at least she and Dare could have time together again without fear of Helen interrupting them.

"So has Helen gone back home to Cambria?"

"No, she's still here for another couple of weeks. That's another reason I want to talk to you."

Oh, God, he wasn't going to ask her to let Helen stay with her, was he? She pushed aside the random thought. Of course he wouldn't do that.

"You and I and what we've been sharing has been great." His somber gaze locked on hers. "But we both knew it was a temporary thing—just while I'm here in town. Now that Helen's here, making it more difficult, it just seems . . . It's probably better to end it now."

Cold gripped Ashley as she stared into his serious, determined eyes. Yes, she'd known it was temporary, but she didn't want it to end now.

"We don't have to stop because Helen is here," she said. "We could meet somewhere else. You could come to my apartment."

"No. It's not just her walking in on us. She's demanding of my attention and . . . well, she has no one else. I can't just turn her away. Surely you understand that. So trying to divide the time between her and you . . . between the business I came here to do . . ." He shrugged. "It wouldn't be fair to you. I just think it's better to end it now."

"And if I don't agree?"

He gazed at her, a light flaring in his eyes, but then it dimmed again and he shook his head.

"I'm sorry." He took her hand and she simultaneously wanted to pull it away and to stay in the warmth of his grip forever. "I think this is for the best."

Ashley closed the door of her apartment behind her, feeling numb. Dare had just broken up with her. Had walked away from what they had without a qualm.

Her stomach clenched and her heart ached. She realized that the growing need she felt for him wasn't just a sexual hunger for the delights of domination he'd introduced her to.

She had developed feelings for him. A deep need for his touch. For him to need her, too.

Could it be that she was in love with Dare?

* * *

Ashley rested her head on Jessica's shoulder as Jessica hugged her. They sat on her couch. Ashley had called Jess right after Dare had dropped her off at her apartment and she'd come right over.

"It's okay, Ashley. That asshole had no right to treat you that way. To just up and ditch you like that. I can't believe he's putting that psycho ahead of you. She's obviously not the person we thought we knew."

"She is his stepdaughter. He's trying to help her," Ashley said, not knowing why she was defending him. This was girl time, when she could dis the guy without guilt and wallow in sharing her pain with her friend.

"Ex-stepdaughter. And no matter what, she's a grown-up now and is responsible for her own actions. If she's going to behave badly, he shouldn't hesitate to boot her out on her butt."

Ashley just nodded. "Which means, he doesn't really care about me." She shook her head. "But I knew that. I can't really blame him. We both knew it was just a temporary thing."

"Oh, you can blame him all you want. He hurt you. You have a right to be angry."

Ashley let a few more tears fall, basking in Jessica's warm hugs, while Jess stroked her hair. Then Ashley sighed and drew away.

"At least now you can finally be with Adam."

"But it's not really fair to Adam that I just latch on to him on the rebound."

Jess smiled. "I think that man would be happy for any reason for you to latch on to him." She stroked Ashley's hair back. "It's not like he's a new guy in your life. You two are friends. You have a deep connection. And you've had the hots for each other for as long as I can remember. Now that he's taken the step of telling you how he feels and wants to move the relationship forward . . ." Jess shrugged. "I don't see why you'd hold back."

Ashley just shook her head, still hurting too much from Dare's rejection to think about it.

"Hey, let's forget about all this right now and just kick back and spend some girl time together," Jess said. "How about I order us a pizza and we follow it up with some Ben and Jerry's while we watch a chick flick? I think Reese Witherspoon has a new one out. Or we can watch a classic. Hey, what about *When Harry Met Sally*? About two friends falling in love?"

Ashley smiled, trying to stop her lip from trembling. "That's a great idea."

Jess dialed her phone and ordered Ashley's favorite, with lots of bacon and mushrooms, and extra cheese. Then she stood up. "I'm going to make a pitcher of 'ritas then go out and get that ice cream."

Ashley grabbed her hand and squeezed. "Thanks, Jess. I really appreciate you being here for me."

"Aw, of course, hon. You'd do the same for me."

Ash smiled. "Yeah, but I won't have to. Because you've found the perfect guy."

Jess had been out on a couple of dates now with Eric and things were definitely heating up between them. And everything Jess told Ash about him showed that he seemed to adore Jess. Ash had a good feeling about the two of them.

It was tough getting up the next morning for work,

after a pitcher of margaritas and staying up way later than she should have. Jess had stayed over and they'd talked half the night. Now they were both regretting the lack of sleep.

But it had been fun.

Thank heavens it was Friday already because she'd definitely be dragging by the end of the day.

Jessica had helped her forget about Dare last night but, at the office, thoughts of him plagued her, keeping her distracted and listless. Her heart still ached thinking about what might have been.

Could she really have believed that he might want to carry on a relationship with her? He'd be returning to New York at the end of the month. What did she think, he'd come visit her every weekend? She'd fly out there and spend time with him?

He might be able to afford to visit her all the time, but her budget wouldn't allow her to do the same. And she couldn't really accept him paying for her travel all the time. As much as she'd love spending weekends in fabulous New York City.

No, it had been a flawed plan all along. Not that she'd really planned it. Her heart just sort of decided it would all work out.

Her heart? Was she really falling for the guy, or was it just the lustful stirrings of her need to be dominated by someone so powerful and authoritative, so sexy and muscular?

Ah, the allure of an older man.

She leaned back in her chair and sighed. Her coffee mug caught her eye. Bold black letters proclaimed HAPPINESS

IS FINISHING YOUR DAILY WORD COUNT above an image of an adorable kitten, fast asleep, with a quill pen lying between its paws. Adam had bought her that cup when she'd confessed to him that she had a secret yearning to be a novelist. He'd been super supportive and had had this mug custom-made for her. Because of its constant reminder on her desk, she wrote a little bit every day, even if it was just a couple hundred words over her lunch hour. She hadn't finished her book yet—she constantly seemed to be revising it—but because of Adam and his encouragement, she was making progress.

Well, right now she needed a coffee. She picked up the mug and headed across the office. When she got to the small room with the coffee machine, she saw that the last person had left the pot nearly empty. She sighed and added coffee grounds to a new filter, then waited while the coffee dribbled into the pot.

She glanced up as someone else stepped into the room.

Adam stood there with his mug in hand.

As soon as Adam saw Ashley standing waiting for the coffeepot to fill, he stopped.

"Oh, sorry, I'll come back later," he said.

Damn it, he missed her. Missed their runs in the morning. Their regular night to get together to watch movies and talk. Even in the office—especially in the office—he'd felt it was important to give her space.

He really shouldn't have come on as strongly as he had that day in his office, but he couldn't undo what he'd done. Now he just had to wait it out to see if she'd come around. Hopefully to embrace the romantic relationship he so hoped they could forge, but even getting back to what they used to have would be a relief.

He wanted her as part of his life, at whatever level she'd allow.

He turned to walk away.

"Wait, Adam. You don't have to go."

He turned back and stepped into the room, taking in the welcome sight of her. But he noticed the dark circles under her eyes. The slight sag of her shoulders. She looked tired. And she seemed to be listless, tapping her fingers against her skirt.

She seemed to be uncomfortable under his gaze.

"So how are you doing?" he asked.

"Fine," she said, but she didn't sound fine. She sounded stressed.

The coffee stopped dripping into the full pot and she picked it up. Another drip splashed on the burner, sizzling softly when it hit the hot metal.

She filled her cup then held up the pot, offering to fill his. He held it out and she poured in the hot coffee.

"Thanks," he said.

She nodded, then turned to grab a milk carton from the fridge. It was unopened and she unfastened the cap and then tugged on the plastic ring of the seal inside. She seemed to be having trouble, then it pulled out and she spilled milk on her skirt.

"Oh, damn." She grabbed a paper towel and started to wipe it up.

"You okay?" Adam asked.

She seemed upset and definitely off her game.

"I'm fine." She poured milk into her coffee then sealed it and put it back in the fridge. "I'm just a bit off today."

He wanted to ask if it was because of him. Did being around him make her this nervous? Or was it something else? If something had happened . . . he wished she felt comfortable talking to him. They'd always shared things before and this distance between them was killing him.

"You know that if you need anything . . . or you just need to talk . . . I'm here for you."

Ashley's heart thumped in her chest. Adam was always there for her. She knew that. But she couldn't talk to him about this. Cry on his shoulder because another man had dumped her. Not when he'd professed his feelings for her.

And if she did tell him, would he jump on the chance to convince her to be with him? And if he did, how hard would it be for him to convince her? When she felt so rejected and fragile? So needy of a man believing she was special?

She knew she could step into his arms and he'd hold her. Tell her everything would be all right. He would tell her how important she was. How much he cared for her. How he always had.

And she would love it. She would give in and succumb to her attraction for him.

But would that be fair to him? Sure, she'd been attracted to Adam for a long time, but she didn't know where it would go. Or if it would last. What if it ended and their friendship along with it?

But mostly it wouldn't be fair to him because she still

had feelings for Dare. And that was no way to start a relationship with Adam.

She stared down at the steam rising from her cup in a slow coiling cloud and nodded.

"I know. Thanks, but I'm fine."

But Ashley was far from fine. She pushed open the door to her apartment and walked inside, dropping her briefcase on the floor beside her. She walked to the couch and slumped down, then pulled off her shoes and tossed them across the room toward the entrance, not caring that they landed several feet short, forming a misshapen mess.

She was tired, and lonely. And she missed Dare.

And Adam.

God, when he'd come into the coffee room and offered to be there for her if she wanted to talk . . . She had so much wanted to take him up on it.

She so much wanted to step into his arms and be held.

She scraped her hair back from her face and rested her head back on the couch. Damn, she had to get a grip.

The phone rang. Thank God.

She snatched up the handset. "Hello?"

"Hi," Jessica said. "I thought I'd check in on you. How are you doing?"

"Oh, God. Adam talked to me today. Said I could talk to him if I needed to."

"You told him Dare broke up with you?"

"No, he just knew something was wrong."

"He's a really great guy."

"Yes, he is. But I'm not calling him." She knew that's what Jessica was trying to get her to do.

"So text him."

"Jess . . ."

"Look, whatever you want to do, but you know I've always thought the two of you would be great together."

"So what are you doing tonight?" Ashley asked, determined to change the subject.

"I'm going out with Eric. But if you want me to come over, I can postpone."

Although she was tempted, she didn't want to ruin Jessica's plans.

"Of course not. I'm fine."

"You sure?"

"Go out with your guy," Ashley insisted. "Then call and tell me all about it tomorrow."

Jessica giggled. "Well, I don't know if I'll tell you *all* about it. But I will call you. Have a good night."

"Yeah, you, too."

Ashley hung up and slumped on the couch again.

She walked to the kitchen and retrieved a half bottle of wine from the fridge and a glass, then settled back on the couch and poured herself some. She took a sip, enjoying the warm sensation in her throat, then the coil of heat in her stomach. She took another sip.

It was going to be a long evening.

Adam grabbed his phone from his suit jacket to check the text message he'd just received. Even though it was after eight, he was still at the office, opting to work late instead of going home and stewing about Ashley.

He glanced at the display, then froze when he saw the text was from Ashley.

Want to come over tonight?

He took a deep breath then typed, *Sure. Are you okay?*

Yeah. A bit lonely. You said we could talk.

His heart soared. She was letting him in again.

Of course, he responded. *I'll be there in half an hour.*

He didn't know why she wasn't with Dare tonight. It was Friday and they only had another few weekends together. But then Dare liked to be in control—Adam knew that only too well—and he liked to keep his partner guessing and a little off balance.

Didn't matter. He was just glad Ashley was free and had asked him to come over.

He cleaned up his desk and locked his office, then headed out of the building, his heart pounding, anticipating being with Ashley again. She was alone and lonely and she'd called on him. He would do everything he could to leverage this in his favor. To win her heart and her body.

Dare walked along the stone path toward the front door of his house. God, he missed Ashley. He wished she was coming over tonight and he could hold her in his arms. Kiss her smooth, sweet skin. Feel her soft hands on him.

He unlocked the door then stepped inside. Helen sat in the living room and stood up when he entered.

After their unfortunate event the other night, she'd slipped out the next day and stayed away. He hadn't known if she'd decided to return home to Cambria or gone to stay with friends, but she'd left her big suitcase behind and a lot of her clothes, so he'd been pretty sure she was still in town. Though you never knew with Helen.

"Dare, I'm sorry about the other night. About getting drunk and . . ." She bit her lip. "For what I did."

This was a good sign. She wasn't calling him *Daddy,* and she actually seemed contrite about what had happened.

"Do you forgive me?" she asked.

"If you really mean it. And if you'll really try to stop drinking again."

"Yes, of course. I really will."

She stepped toward him and wrapped her arms around his waist, giving him a hug. He relented and wrapped his arms around her, too.

Then she gazed up at him, her head resting on his shoulder.

"You know I love you," she said.

"I love you, too, Helen. And I'll always be there for you."

"I'm glad. But I don't mean like a stepdaughter. I knew Mom wasn't right for you. And she didn't deserve you. But I would be so good for you. I'd do anything you want. I'd be the best possible wife, and—"

"Wife?" He stepped back, disentangling himself from her arms. "Helen, listen to yourself. You are my ex-stepdaughter, and that's all our relationship is. I care about you, but I have no romantic feelings here. I know you have a need for stability, and to have a strong father image in your life permanently. But this isn't the way."

"No, I want *you.* It has nothing to do with any of that other stuff."

"Don't keep pushing this, Helen. It's never going to happen and if you persist, it will destroy the relationship we do have."

She frowned, her eyes glittering in anger. "And yet you'll fuck that tramp Ashley. Who is exactly the same age as me." Her eyes flared with rage.

"That's not the same."

"Really? I don't see the difference." She planted her hands on her hips. "So will she wind up being my new stepmother?"

"The relationship between Ashley and me is none of your business."

Helen huffed out a loud sigh. "So you don't really care about me. And you never have."

"That's not true."

But he was talking to her back as she stormed across the room and then down the hall. He heard her door slam behind her.

He clenched his fists. Damn it. He was tempted to just throw his exasperating ex-stepdaughter out the door and lock it behind her. He'd faced a lot of challenges in his life, but trying to help Helen seemed to be a losing battle and he wondered if it was worth continuing the fight.

He raked his hand through his hair. He'd given up Ashley because of Helen's intrusion into his life again, and his desire to help her.

Had he been a fucking idiot?

Adam was hungry and he had no idea if Ashley had eaten yet, so he decided to grab some Chinese food to take over with him. He arrived at the entrance to her apartment building and went into the atrium, then buzzed her apartment.

Moments later, he was riding the elevator up to her

ninth-floor apartment. He walked down the hall then tapped on the door. He heard her call to come in and he opened it. She was rushing across the living room toward him, wearing a colorful fleece robe.

When she reached him, her arms went around his waist and her body crushed against him. He dropped the bag with the Chinese food and wrapped his arms around her, too. At the feel of her soft breasts pressed against him, he could tell she wasn't wearing a bra, which caused his body to tighten, but beneath the fabric he could feel a strap around her torso.

Then her lips found his and his heart raced. Her soft mouth moved on his, her tongue stroking the seam of his lips. He opened, welcoming her in. Her tongue dipped into his mouth, her delicate exploration making his cock swell.

She tasted of wine and his gaze swept to where she'd been sitting in the living room. There was a nearly empty bottle of wine and a single glass.

He drew back. Shit. Her warm welcome had made him think that tonight might be the start of something new and special between them. Romantic. Sexual. Fulfilling.

But if she'd been drinking . . .

"I'm so glad you came over," she said, her head pressed against his chest. He stroked her hair from her face.

"Of course. Is everything all right?"

She gazed up at him, her soulful eyes gleaming with sadness. "It's over between Dare and me."

She took his hand and tugged him forward. He grabbed the bag, then let her lead him to the living room.

"I'm sorry, Ash." He placed the bag on the coffee table as she turned around.

"No you aren't, but that's okay. I know it's because you care about me." She slid into his arms again and he couldn't help but hold her close and enjoy the play of her lips on his again.

"Yes, I do, and that's why I need to back off right now."

Her eyes widened as she gazed up at him. "But, why?" Her hand flattened on his chest and stroked downward. Very slowly. Sending heat wafting through his body as she neared his growing cock.

He planted his hand on top of hers, stopping its travels. "Ash . . . sweetheart . . . it looks like you've had a lot to drink." He eased away from her soft body. "There's no way I'd take advantage of the situation."

He gestured to the nearly empty wine bottle on the coffee table.

She glanced around then turned back to him. "I've had two glasses, that's all. That's the bottle left over from the last time you were here for dinner."

He remembered they hadn't finished the wine that night and . . . yes, two glasses would be about right.

His gaze fell to her wide eyes. Damn, this was really happening.

Excitement surged through him and he grabbed her and pulled her into his arms. His lips captured hers and he drove his tongue into her mouth, reveling in the velvety softness. She melted against him, her heart pounding just as fast as his.

His mouth lifted from hers. Now he understood why she'd looked so stressed in the coffee room today.

"When did it happen?" he asked.

"A couple of days ago."

"Why didn't you tell me?"

"I knew you'd want to move forward with a relationship and . . ."

"You aren't ready?"

"I didn't want to approach you on the rebound. That didn't seem fair to you." She stroked his chest, her delicate touch stoking his desire.

He didn't have to ask her why she had called him tonight. The hunger in her eyes said it all.

He laughed, then tightened his arms around her. "I don't care how I get you. Rebound or not." He stroked her soft cheek gently with his thumb. "I believe this has always been inevitable."

She tipped up her head and brushed her lips against his in a long, lingering kiss, so sweet it almost brought tears to his eyes. His greatest fantasy was about to come true. He was finally going to be with this wonderful woman.

"I'm glad," she murmured softly against his lips. "Because the thought of you dominating me like you promised in your office has me so hot I can barely stop from going up in flames."

He gazed down at her, seeing the impish glint in her eyes.

He grinned broadly. "Really?"

She stepped back and stood in the center of the room. "You do want to dominate me?" She smiled seductively. "Don't you?"

Before he could answer, she opened her robe and dropped it to the ground, revealing an erotic, barely-there leather getup. Her body seemed to be covered with black, leather straps wound around her torso, but nothing seemed to be covered. His gaze fell on her full, round breasts, totally exposed to his view. He hardened at the sight of her. Her pussy was covered by a small triangle of leather, but when she turned around in front of him, he could see that her round, firm ass was totally exposed.

God, her body was glorious. His gaze traveled from her very full breasts with tightly peaked nipples, to her long, slender torso, over the curve of her hips, then down her long, shapely legs. She was barefoot, but her toes were polished a shiny, rich crimson.

She turned and leaned over, giving him a delightful view of her round, firm ass. She pulled some shoes out from a drawer in her coffee table, then stood up. As soon as she stepped into the stilettos, her legs appeared even longer and her ass higher and firmer.

"Do you want me submissive, or willful?" she asked.

His cock lurched at the idea of having to subdue her. Of pushing her up against the wall and forcing her hands above her head, then pinning her against the hard surface with his body. His cock twitched at the thought of him pressing his groin hard against her, his shaft cushioned against her soft body.

But they had time. He could play out that scenario another time. Maybe in his office.

His cock twitched.

Right now he wanted her focused on his pleasure. On *their* pleasure. Just as he'd be focused on hers.

"Submissive," he said.

She smiled, then dropped her gaze to the floor and knelt in front of him. "Whatever you command, sir."

He didn't quite know how to start. All he knew was, with her kneeling on the floor in front of him, practically naked, he had to free his throbbing, aching cock from the too-tight confines of his jeans.

He unzipped his pants, then released his hard shaft from the fabric.

"Look at me, Ash."

Ash raised her gaze to see Adam standing before her, his cock a long, hard spike protruding from his jeans.

"Look at what you've done to me."

His cock was thick and hard, the head large and deep red. It seemed to pulse with life as veins rippled along the length of the shaft. She licked her lips, longing to run her tongue over his hot, hard flesh.

Seeing the invitation in her eyes, he stepped closer.

He rested his hand on the top of her head, then glided down the back. He drew her forward until her lips touched the tip of his cock. She opened. He didn't push forward, so she licked his tip, tasting the salty drop of precum already oozing from him.

She pressed her lips to him and swirled her tongue over the tip, then widened her mouth around him.

"Oh, God, Ash." He drew her forward and she took in his whole cockhead, the thick flesh filling her mouth.

She sucked on him, to his groans. His hand stroked over her hair. She moved further forward, taking his cock deeper into her mouth. It was thick and firm between her lips and she dragged her tongue along the smooth skin as she glided forward. Slowly.

She moved forward and back in short strokes, then lengthened them, taking him deeper, then short again.

"Fuck, Ash." He groaned, his hand tightening on her head. "I can't believe we're doing this."

His hand tightened on the crown of her head and he guided her, setting a rhythm. His cock slid in and out of her mouth, sending heat throbbing through her. She could feel the slickness between her thighs, readying her for him.

One of her hands was wrapped tightly around the base of his cock, squeezing as she took him deep into her mouth. She glided the other hand to the button of his jeans and unfastened it, then slid inside. When she cupped his balls in her palm, he groaned.

He was close. She could feel the tension in his body, his cock pulsing in her mouth. His balls hardening in her hand.

She drew her mouth from the tip of his cock. "I want to make you come, sir. In my mouth. I want to swallow everything you give me."

He groaned and as soon as she took his erection in her mouth again, he pulled her tight to his groin. He rocked his pelvis against her, his whole body trembling, but then he coiled his hand in her hair and slowly dragged her head back.

"Baby, I want to come inside you, but not your mouth. Not this time."

He pulled on her hair, easing her to her feet.

"And I'm the one in charge. Right?"

"Yes, sir."

She quivered at the glittering confidence in his eyes.

She reached down and grasped the triangle of leather covering her folds, then tore it away, the snaps giving at her sharp motion. His gaze dropped to her intimate flesh, desire filling his eyes.

Then she turned and leaned over the back of the couch, offering herself to him. His hand rested on her ass and he stroked. Over the curve and around to her hip. Gliding to her inner thigh, grazing the sensitive flesh, only a breath from her aching opening, then away again.

"You are so fucking sexy leaned over like that. Your pussy glistening with need."

Oh, God, those words coming from Adam, whom she'd wanted for so long, as he gazed at her vulnerable, exposed flesh, sent ripples of need through her.

"Please touch me, sir. Please drive your big cock into me."

He chuckled. "Oh, I will. There's no doubt about that. But I'm not going to take you bent over a couch. I want our bodies joined, not just my cock inside you. And I want to see your face."

His hands wrapped around her waist and he pulled her to a standing position. His lips nuzzled her ear, sending spasms of pleasure quivering through her, as his hands wandered over her body. He cupped her naked breast and her hard, swollen nipple pressed into his palm as he stroked. When his fingertips found her sensitive nub and squeezed, piercing shards of desire lanced through her. She arched against his hand, moaning. She could feel his smile against her neck.

His other hand glided down her belly, then . . .

"Oh, God, yes." Her voice cracked as his fingers slid over her folds, grazing them lightly, then stroking more thoroughly.

When two fingers slid inside her, she moaned softly. His thumb found her clit as his fingers explored her inner passage. She leaned back against his big body, helpless against the onslaught of pleasure. Afraid her knees would buckle and she'd crumple to the floor.

"Turn around," he murmured in her ear.

She obeyed, rotating within his arms until she faced him. The heat in his dark brown eyes took her breath away. He slid his hand under her knee and lifted, easing her back until her ass perched on the back of the couch.

When she felt his blunt tip brush her sensitive flesh, she held her breath.

"I'm going to enter you now. My cock is going to slide deep inside you."

She just stared at him, her eyes wide, and nodded.

"Do you want that?" he asked.

"Oh, yes, please." The need in her voice shocked her, and brought a smile to his face.

"Good."

Then the pressure of his cockhead against her opening increased. Her soft flesh resisted at first, then as he pushed forward, it opened, gliding around him, welcoming him inside. The feel of his shaft gliding into her, the thickness opening her wide, sent a thrill through her.

This was Adam. His big body possessing hers. As she'd dreamed of for so long.

She moaned as he pushed deeper, stroking her aching passage with every inch. Driving her need higher.

"Do you like that, Ash?"

"Oh, God, yes. I love you inside me."

He laughed out loud, the rumbling in his chest vibrating through her. His cock still filling her. She squeezed him and he groaned, then surged the rest of the way in.

He held her tight to him, their bodies joined, and they both sucked in air.

"Fuck, I can't believe I'm finally inside you. You're so soft and warm around me."

"And you are so hard and thick."

He tipped her head up and covered her mouth with his. It was a gentle kiss, but then his tongue pulsed into her mouth and she suckled it, trying to pull it deeper.

His cock twitched inside her and he tore his mouth away.

"Fuck, Ash, you're going to end this too soon." He stroked her cheek, his gaze solemn. "I want this to be perfect. For both of us."

She gazed into his gleaming eyes. "It is perfect."

He smiled. "No, I'll show you perfect."

He drew back, his hard cock stroking her on its journey out, then just as it seemed he would drop from her body, he surged forward again.

She clung to him. "Oh, yes."

Then he drew back and glided deep again.

Pleasure washed through her, rippling along her nerve endings.

He drew her knee higher and pulsed into her again. She quivered at the feel of his iron-hard flesh filling her.

He filled her again. And again. His strokes became thrusts and she moaned at the building bliss.

He nibbled her neck, his lips playing over her sensitive flesh.

She moaned, feeling the building heat inside her. Knowing an orgasm was only a breath away.

"Are you close, baby?" he murmured against her ear, his soft breath almost enough to drive her over the edge.

"Oh, yes. Make me come."

"Not yet." He slowed his strokes, to her whimper. "Don't come until I tell you."

His cock slid deep, sending her dangerously close to the precipice.

But she would heed his command.

"Wrap your legs around me."

As she opened her legs wider, his thick, hard cock burrowed deeper inside her and she groaned. She shuddered in his arms as he carried her across the apartment.

"Don't come, baby," he murmured against her ear, but the feel of his thick shaft jostling inside her as he walked made it almost impossible to obey his request.

Almost. But she gritted her teeth and breathed deeply.

Finally, he set her on her bed, then leaned her back.

He smiled, a devilish glint in his brown eyes. "You can barely hold it back," he said with smug satisfaction in his voice. Then he nuzzled her ear, sending waves of sensation rippling through her. Every nerve ending was on alert, quivering with need.

"Don't worry. I'll make sure it's worth it."

Then he drew back and thrust forward. At the feel of his thick cock dragging along her inner passage, then driving deep again, she groaned, her body shuddering with need. Then he did it again.

She clung to him, her head rolling back on the bed, her eyelids closing as she lost herself in the heady sensations.

"Open your eyes, baby. I want to watch you when you come."

Her eyelids flickered open and she found herself gazing into his intense dark chocolate eyes. Their gazes locked and she felt like they were bonded together. Body. Mind. And soul. She could no more look away than she could stop her heart from beating.

He thrust into her again and she shuddered. Pleasure blossomed inside her, deep in her core, then rippled across every nerve ending. His next thrust released the tightly coiled need inside her, and joy exploded inside her in an earth-shattering, mind-numbing orgasm.

He cupped her head and held her gaze. "Say my name."

"Adam . . ." She moaned as the orgasm battered through her in a rush of pleasure. She clung to him, their gazes still locked together. "Oh, God, yes. Adam."

At the sound of his name on a long moan, he groaned, then drove deep into her, pinning her to the bed with his body . . . and she felt it. His cock pulsed inside her, then hot liquid filled her, flooding her insides.

She held him tight as the two of them gasped for air. "Oh, God, that was incredible."

He chuckled. "And, baby, it's not over yet."

He slid down her body then to his knees beside the bed. Then he licked her, oblivious of their shared fluids dripping from her body and she trembled at the exquisite pleasure of his tongue dragging over her sensitive clit. She arched, her body sensitized and quivering at the edge of another orgasm. Then she felt it. A surge of pleasure from deep inside her rising, shuddering through her body, then blasting through her in a heated wave of blissful sensations. She clung to him as she seemed to shatter into a million pieces.

Ashley sipped her coffee as she stared at the Sunday crossword puzzle. Adam had spent all day Saturday with her . . . and Saturday night. He had taken her fast and hard against the wall, then later made tender, passionate love to her in bed. She smiled at the memory. Then they'd gone for a run this morning and he'd headed home.

She had all day Sunday to get a few chores done, then just relax and forget about everything stressful until she returned to work tomorrow.

Then she'd have to continue working on her article. The one Dare had been helping her with.

Unsettling feelings stirred inside her at thoughts of Dare. She sipped her steaming coffee again. She had started a relationship with Adam now. One she knew she'd be happy in. He was perfect for her.

Why then did thoughts of Dare still make her ache inside? She'd always known there was no future there. Even though she'd kidded herself for a while that maybe it could happen.

But that hope had been shattered by him. He'd never wanted any more from her than a few weeks of fucking. She was probably just an amusing distraction, but then she'd become inconvenient when Helen had shown up.

Bitter, spiteful Helen.

She was his ex-stepdaughter, and clearly he still thought of her as family and his responsibility.

Which was commendable, she had to admit.

Her buzzer sounded and she hopped up, wondering if it was Adam. Maybe he hadn't been able to get enough of her and had come back to spend the afternoon. She grinned broadly. She was definitely up for some afternoon delight.

"Yes?" she said into the speaker.

"A delivery for Ms. Cane."

A delivery? "I'm sorry, I'm not expecting anything," she answered.

"Hey, lady, I have flowers here for you. Long-stemmed red roses."

Adam had sent her flowers? She pushed the button, a smile spreading across her face.

She waited impatiently for the knock on the door. He seemed to take forever to arrive, but finally, as she peered out the peephole, she saw the man carrying a large arrangement of huge red roses in a tall vase, surrounded by cellophane. She pulled open the door and took the flowers from him.

"Oh, wait, I need to grab my purse."

"The tip's already taken care of. He said not to let you worry about that." Then the guy turned and walked down the hall.

She pushed the door closed with her foot, holding the arrangement with both hands and breathing in the sweet fragrance. Baby's breath and lacy greenery accented the flowers, all standing in a stunning crystal vase.

She carried it to the dining room table and pulled open the clear plastic. The flowers were exquisite, the tight red blossoms just beginning to open. She glanced around for a card but couldn't find one.

A knock sounded at the door again. Had the delivery guy forgotten something? She walked to the door and opened it. Then her eyes widened at the sight of another delivery man with another vase of roses.

"There must be some mistake," she said. "I already received some roses."

The guy smiled. "No mistake, ma'am."

She took the new vase of flowers and set it on the table beside the first one. Then there was another knock at the door. She opened it to the sight of yet another delivery man with flowers.

"Oh my God." But she took them and set them on the coffee table.

At the next knock she was no longer surprised. She took the next vase and put them in her bedroom on the dresser.

There were several more deliveries, until she had ten vases of flowers scattered around her small apartment. The place was filled with the delightful fragrance of the roses.

As she carried the latest vase to the kitchen, she realized this one had a card. She plucked the small pink envelope from the plastic holder, then opened it with a smile.

But as soon as she saw the inside of the card, her breath caught. The name at the bottom wasn't Adam's scrawled signature. The writing was bold and tightly controlled. And read, *Dare.*

She sank into the chair. The note said:

You are as beautiful as these flowers and far more precious. I never should have let you go.

Shock vaulted through her. Dare had changed his mind?

She stomped down her rising hope, not wanting to convince herself it was true only to find that he only meant these flowers as an apology for hurting her, or he was just trying to cheer her up because he felt guilty for ditching her.

Another knock sounded on her door. She walked to the entrance.

"Not more flowers," she said as she opened the door. Then her heart leaped.

Dare stood in the hallway. His blue-and-white-striped shirt and lean jeans showcased his powerful frame and the musky scent of his cologne released unsettling memories of his body close to her in more intimate situations.

"May I come in?" His deep, sexy voice tugged at her emotions.

She wanted to hear her name on his lips. To have him whisper it in her ear, then nuzzle her neck.

She stepped aside to let him in, not trusting her voice.

"I see you got my flowers." He smiled, and the charming gleam in his eye was almost her undoing.

She wanted to throw herself in his arms and tell him how much she wanted him. How much she loved him. But how could she admit that when she didn't know if she believed it herself? Was her attraction to him just her need for a father figure? Didn't that make her just like Helen? Couldn't that have been part of the reason he broke up with her?

"What did you mean by the card?"

"I thought it was very clear."

He stepped toward her and she had to stop herself from backing away. His hands held on to her shoulders, gripping them firmly.

"I made a mistake. I don't want to end what we had."

"What about Helen?"

"I can't let her dictate my life. She may have problems, and I'll help her solve them, but that shouldn't get in the way of my happiness."

He drew her close and wrapped his arms around her, holding her close in a gentle embrace. "And you make me happy," he murmured, then nuzzled her ear.

Delightful sensations rippled along her skin.

"I do?"

He gazed at her, a smile spreading across his face. "Yes, you do." He tipped up her chin and brushed his lips against hers in a sweet, poignant kiss.

"My big mistake was thinking that we had to end this when my business is done here. That might be what you want, but I hope to find a way to convince you otherwise."

"You thought that's what I want?" She shook her head. "I thought that's what you wanted."

A chuckle rumbled from his chest and he smiled broadly. "So does that mean we can continue what we started?"

Her heart soared and she smiled so wide her cheeks hurt. "Yes."

She wrapped her arms around his neck and kissed him, her lips moving on his in a passionate, consuming kiss. Her tongue pushed into his mouth and she tasted cinnamon and coffee. His tongue tangled with hers, their bodies so tight she could feel his pounding heart. Or was that hers?

Then he swept her up in his arms and carried her to

the couch. He set her down and glided the hem of her top upward. She sucked in a breath and grabbed his hand, stopping him.

Oh, God, how could she have forgotten about Adam?

"No, we can't."

"Why not?"

"I . . ." She bit her lip as she stared into his midnight blue eyes. "I'm involved with someone now."

Dare frowned. "You started seeing someone else?"

She nodded.

"This would be the friend you were telling me about that you have feelings for."

"That's right."

"Fuck, are you kidding me? We've only been apart a few days."

"And he and I have been attracted for years."

"Yet you've never done anything about this attraction before. So why now?"

She dragged her fingernail along the armrest of the couch, staring intently at the fabric. "Well, because of you. When I started seeing you, it made us realize that the barriers keeping us apart—the age difference, the fact that he's my boss—don't really matter."

Wait a minute. He was her boss? She was involved with Adam Rawlins?

Fuck, why did it have to be Adam?

Adam watched Ashley working studiously at her desk as he approached. He'd been dying to see her since he'd left her on Sunday morning. Wanting to hold her in his arms again. To feel her soft hair against his cheek. He wanted to taste her sweet mouth as he plundered her lips.

And he didn't want to wait until this evening to do it.

"Ashley," he said as he stood facing her desk.

She glanced up, startled. "Oh, Adam. Good morning."

Her voice sounded strained and her gaze flickered away from his. Was she nervous about their relationship in the office? Maybe she was hoping they'd keep it quiet.

"I need to see you in my office," he said, keeping his boss face on.

"Okay." She stood up and followed him to his door.

Once inside, he turned. "Close the door."

She closed it, then with a stern expression on his face, as if he'd called her in here to lecture her, he walked toward her. Slowly.

"I heard about something that happened this weekend."

She gazed at him uncertainly. "You did?"

"That's right. About you and a man."

Her eyes widened. She shook her head. "I . . ."

God, she seemed nervous.

"You know, office romances can be tricky things." He stopped in front of her and stroked her cheek. "But you and I have history, and a deep friendship. I know we'll be fine. But if you want to keep it quiet for a while, then we can do that."

"Is that what *you* want?"

"Hell, no. I'm happy to shout it from the rooftops." He grinned. "We could put it on the front page of the magazine."

He pulled her into his arms and kissed her, gliding his

tongue deep into her mouth and stroking until he felt her melt against him. His hand slid to the small of her back and he pulled her tight to his hips, his cock already growing for her. Ready to slide inside her.

He spun her around and backed her to the wall, then pressed her to it. He continued to kiss her, her head pressed to the wall as he grabbed her wrists and drew them over her head, then pinned them there with one hand.

She seemed to struggle a bit against him and his cock twitched. The thought of her resisting him . . . of him having to subdue her . . . God, his cock hardened to a steel column. Role-playing with her was going to be fan-fucking-tastic.

He cupped her breast, then stroked down her body. He pivoted his hips against her so she could feel how hard he was, then he grabbed a handful of her flowing, floral skirt and drew it upward.

She shook her head, dislodging their lips.

"No, Adam. Please."

He frowned as he saw the panic in her eyes.

"Sorry, Ash." He released her skirt, but still held her hands and body in place, then grinned. "I just wanted to make good on my promise to dominate you in my office."

Then he kissed her again, his lips persuasive on hers, and her stiff body relaxed. Then he glided his tongue into her mouth. Gently this time. Caressing.

She murmured and even arched a little against him. He could feel her nipples, like hard beads pushing through the fabric.

But as soon as he drew away his mouth and smiled down at her, she said, "Please let me go. We need to talk."

The words were like a knife to the heart. Nothing good ever came from those words.

But he knew he was overreacting. He and Ash had finally gotten past all the obstacles to their happiness. She was his now. He'd shared the delights of her body while they'd shared intense, incredible pleasure together.

This was their happily-ever-after. There was no way this could be the end.

Ashley stared at Adam's face. Uncertainty flickered through his warm, brown eyes.

Oh, God, she didn't know what to say now. What to do. But she couldn't let this continue without saying something.

She remembered that Adam had been in a serious relationship years ago, just after she and Jessica had left for college. Ashley had never met the woman who'd hurt Adam, but he had been devastated when she'd left him and as a result, he'd only had a couple of relationships in the handful of years since then. She knew he was afraid of having his heart broken again, and she definitely didn't want to be the one who did that.

"Are you dumping me?" he asked as he stepped back, giving her room to breathe.

"No, it's not like that." She sidestepped him and walked to one of the two chairs by his small, round meeting table, then sat down.

He sat across from her. "What is it, then?"

She folded her hands on the tabletop. "A few hours after you left yesterday . . . in the afternoon . . ." She was aware of his intense scrutiny while he waited for her explanation. She sighed. "Dare came to see me."

"What?" Anger flared in his eyes. "Why? I thought it was over between you."

She nodded. "I thought so, too, but . . ." She forced herself to hold his gaze. "He told me he wants to get back together again."

Adam snorted. "Back together? You were never really together. He just fucked you a couple of times."

"Adam . . ."

He stood up. "No, really, Ash. Don't tell me you're considering this. It isn't real for him. He doesn't have feelings for you. You're just a distraction from his busy life. Believe me, when his business is done here, he'll be gone and all you'll have left is a broken heart."

The pain in his eyes made her realize that he was remembering the agony he'd suffered after losing the woman he'd loved.

"No, he said he wants more than that. He wants to keep seeing me even after. He said we can make it work."

The pain in his eyes turned to simmering anger. "So that's it? He beckons and you're just going to drop what we could have?" He took her hand and squeezed, the warmth of his fingers around hers tugging on her heart. "After all this time when we've clearly wanted each other . . ." He lifted her hand to his mouth and his lips brushed lightly across her skin. "Can you really give up what we have so easily?"

She shook her head, her heart crushing. "Adam, it's not easy."

* * *

Adam's heart froze. Fuck, this was it. She was going to walk away. The remembered pain of abandonment from last time . . . the only other time he'd allowed himself to love . . .

"Oh, Adam, no." Ashley's soft hand rested against his cheek. "I didn't mean . . ." She drew in a deep breath. "What I meant was, there's nothing about this situation that's easy." She stroked his cheek. "You are my close friend and what we shared this weekend was amazing—"

"But?"

She shook her head. "No buts. I don't want to end what we have between us."

His eyes lit with hope.

"But I also have to honor the fact that . . ." She pursed her lips. "Well, I have feelings for Dare." As she gazed into Adam's anxious brown eyes, she knew she had to tell him the whole truth. "I think I'm falling in love with him."

He drew her hand away from his face. "Fuck, so how is this not ending it with me?"

She frowned. "Because, Adam, I think I'm in love with you, too."

Part Three

"You think you're in love with both of us?" Adam's heart ached as he stared at her. "Me and Dare?" He shook his head. "I don't believe that. I think what you feel for him is just infatuation, and when that runs its course, you'll wind up with nothing."

She shook her head. "No, you're wrong. What I feel for you both is deeper than infatuation." She bit her lip. "This is so difficult."

"It doesn't have to be." He took both her hands and gazed deep into her eyes. "Just choose me."

"It's not that simple."

"It is. You and I have history. A solid friendship, which is a great foundation for a relationship. You know me. Know that together we can make things work. All you know about him is that he's going to leave. Even if you continue your relationship after that, he lives in New York and you live here. Are you going to give up your job and move there?"

His gut clenched at the thought. There would be great opportunities for her in New York and Dare could make them happen for her. With his wealth and connections, he could open doors. He could probably call up a friend and have her working at a big magazine within a week, if he wanted. Even if she started as a copy editor or fact-checker, she would quickly prove herself capable of being a leading journalist. She was a good worker and a talented writer.

"I'm not thinking about any of that right now." She frowned. "But I don't think I want to go to New York. I don't want to leave Autumn's Ridge and all my friends." She gazed into his eyes, her own blue ones filled with sadness. "Or you."

His heart soared. She did care about him. He just had to convince her.

He pulled her into his arms and captured her lips, all the love and need he felt for her flowing through him, infusing the kiss with persuasive passion.

Her soft body conformed to his as she returned the kiss, her mouth moving on his, her tongue stroking his.

Their lips parted and he gazed at her, everything he felt for her shining in his eyes.

"I love you, Ashley." He hadn't said the words yet. But she knew. He knew she did.

She rested her hand on his cheek. "And I love you, too. But that doesn't change how I feel about him." She drew back. "I'm sorry, but I need time to think. To figure this whole thing out."

"And in the meantime you'll keep seeing him?" Adam demanded. "Keep fucking him?" Anger simmered through him.

"Adam . . ."

"I'm sorry. That was uncalled for." He shook his head. "I just don't want to lose you."

"I know." She took his hand and squeezed. "Just give me time. I'll figure this out."

"Just one question, Ash. Does Dare know about us and my feelings for you?"

She bit her lip. "I told him I'm seeing someone, but he doesn't know I'm in love with either one of you."

Adam nodded. He felt a small sense of satisfaction that he was the first of the two of them she'd told.

"And does he know who I am?"

"No, he just knows you're a friend of mine. There was no reason to elaborate."

"And, as I mentioned before, I sensed there was some tension between you two after your internship at his company so I didn't tell him it was you."

When he was at college, studying communications, he'd needed an internship in the fall of his third year so Ashley's brother had asked Ash to ask Helen to put in a word for him with Dare. Dare had a big company and got him a position writing copy for the marketing department.

"Do you think he'd remember you?" she asked.

"It doesn't really matter, does it?"

Of course, she had no idea that Dare had taken a special interest in Adam. Adam was a friend of his step-daughter's. Even though Adam and Helen didn't know each other very well—they were connected only by the fact that he was a friend of her friend's brother—Dare took Helen's request to help Adam seriously. He'd wanted to ensure Adam was happy in the position and getting the most out of it he could.

And it was during that fall that Dare had gone through one of the most traumatic times of his life.

"When are you seeing him next?" Adam asked.

"In two days."

Adam just nodded. It was time he went and paid Dare a visit.

Adam pulled up in front of the gray brick house that he knew Dare was staying in while he was here in Autumn's Ridge. It wasn't the same place he'd owned when he used to live here. That had been sold off after the divorce. Apparently, according to Ashley, this was a new place Dare had bought some years later. Dare had business holdings in town, but Adam hadn't thought Dare made enough trips to town to warrant having a house here, but then Adam didn't really know much about Dare's comings and goings.

All he knew was that Dare had never made a move to contact him.

And that hurt.

He got out of the car and walked up the stone path, breathing in the sweet scent of lilacs. Ash loved lilacs. Every time she came here, that fragrance was bound to delight her.

Once at the entrance, he drew in a deep breath, then rang the doorbell. His stomach tightened as he waited for Dare to open the door.

How would Dare react to seeing Adam on the other side of the door? What would he say?

He saw a shadow through the beveled and frosted glass design on the door. He braced himself as the door opened.

Helen stared at him, her eyes wide. Then she frowned.

"What are you doing here?" Her acerbic tone grated.

"I'm here to see Dare."

"Well, he's not in." Then she slammed the door in his face.

He stood staring at the door as her shadowy shape disappeared inside the house.

"What the hell was that all about?" Dare asked as Helen marched past. When he'd heard the male voice at the door, asking to see him, he'd put down his newspaper and walked toward the foyer, only to see Helen slam the door.

"It was no one."

Well, that was a lie.

"Helen, I don't need you filtering who I see."

"Whatever," she called as she stormed down the hall to her room.

He opened the front door. Standing on the other side was Adam.

His gut clenched. God, he didn't think it would be this hard seeing him again.

"Hello, Dare."

"Adam."

"Helen doesn't seem very happy to see me."

Dare gripped the doorknob tighter. "She'll get over it."

"I'm here to talk about Ashley."

Dare nodded. "I'm not surprised."

"So you do know I'm the other man she's seeing?"

"Not the whole time. Just since the other day when she told me she'd been seeing her boss."

Adam frowned and Dare could just hear the cogs in his brain turning. Dare hadn't contacted Adam in all these years since . . . painful memories tore through him and he gritted his teeth as he pushed them aside . . . but he'd kept tabs on Adam. He'd wanted to know that he was all right. That his life was going well.

That he was happy.

This mess with Ashley sure put a crimp in that.

"May I come in?" Adam asked, still standing in the cool evening air, waiting.

Dare glanced over his shoulder, thinking of Helen brooding in her room. Just waiting to be a pain in the ass if he and Adam came inside to talk.

He gazed at Adam, really looking at him for the first time since he'd opened the door. God, he looked good. He could see the hint of sculpted muscle through the T-shirt he wore and his arms were well defined. His chestnut brown hair was swept back from his handsome face and his dark brown eyes were still as deep and haunting as Dare remembered.

And just as full of pain.

"I think it's better if we go out somewhere." And for more reasons than Helen's probability of being a nuisance. Being alone with Adam would be too painful. And too . . . tempting. "How about a drink at Wanabee's?"

He grabbed his keys from the bowl by the door, then stepped outside. "We can take my car if you like."

"I'll meet you there."

Whether Adam didn't want to be in the close quarters

of a small car with Dare, or he just didn't want to come all the way back here afterward to pick up his car, Dare didn't know, but it was probably just as well. Being that close to Adam would definitely be a strain.

Ten minutes later, Dare parked his car behind Adam's gray sedan in front of the upscale bar and got out. Adam waited for him at the door, then they went inside.

"A quiet booth," Dare told the hostess.

"Of course, sir." She led them to a booth on a quiet side of the place.

Adam slid into the booth across from Dare. No wonder Ash was so taken by him. His dark, almost black hair was cropped short on the sides but long enough on top to showcase the thick waves. His square jaw was shadowed with coarse whiskers and his smoldering deep blue eyes were even sexier than he remembered. Maybe the extra years had added an even stronger sense of authority behind them.

"You still like gin and tonic?" Dare asked.

Adam shook his head. "Heineken," he told the waitress.

"Same," Dare said.

"So are you going to ask why I left five years ago? And why I never looked you up since then?" Dare asked.

The waitress approached the table with a round tray holding two green beer bottles and two tall glasses. She placed them on the table, then poured each beer into a glass.

Once she'd gone, Dare leaned toward Adam. "I never meant to hurt you."

At Dare's words, pain vibrated through every cell of Adam's being, but he wouldn't let himself be dragged down that road.

"I don't care about that. I'm here to talk about what's happening between you and Ashley."

Adam watched Dare sip from his tall glass. His expression barely changed—the man had almost perfect control over his expression at all times—but Adam had gotten to know Dare better than most people and could see the caution there.

"My impression was that you know what's happening with Ash and me. You're her boss so you know she's coming to me for research on an article." He stared at his glass. "I'm the real-life Christian Grey, right?"

"But you've taken it past research with her. You've made her your sub. You're having sex with her." Adam clenched his teeth at the thought, anger vibrating through him. "You don't seem to care that she's going to get hurt."

"I'm not beating her, you know?"

"What?" Adam couldn't help but think about Ashley bent over, her lovely round ass bare and exposed, then the flat of Dare's strong hand smacking it. Then the creamy flesh turning pink.

"Like Christian Grey. I'm not flogging Ashley."

"You've read the books?" Adam asked in surprise.

"No. But I saw the movie." Dare shrugged. "Curiosity."

Adam's lips compressed. "Whatever. That's not what I'm talking about. You're going to hurt Ashley when you walk away. But I guess you've never cared before, so why start now?"

"Look, Adam, what happened between you and me—"

"I said I don't want to talk about that," Adam said through gritted teeth.

"Fine." Dare sighed. "The point is, I don't intend to walk away from Ashley."

"Then what about me and my feelings?" Adam leaned forward. "I'm in love with her."

"And how does she feel about you?"

"She says she loves me, too."

Dare's eyes narrowed. "If she told you that, and she's not here breaking up with me, then I bet she also confessed she's in love with me, too."

Adam frowned. "The decent thing for you to do would be to walk away right now."

"And hurt Ash exactly the way you've been accusing me of?"

"She'll get over it."

"You mean, she'll get over you when she chooses me."

Adam arched a brow. "You're very sure of yourself."

"Of course. And that's exactly why she'll pick me over you. I know you've told her you can dominate her just as well as me, but we both know that's not true."

Adam couldn't deny that. The man had six years on him and ran a huge corporation. He was used to making multimillion-dollar decisions that could make or break whole companies and people's lives. He also had a lot more practice being a Dom. If it came down to sheer ability to dominate, Dare would win hands-down.

"Maybe. But Ash and I have friendship. And a deep caring for each other. We could build a long and happy life together."

Dare raised an eyebrow. "You're talking marriage? It's a little soon to be thinking about that, isn't it?"

"Not for me. I know that's where it's headed for Ash and me. I know we'll be able to make it work. Can you say the same?"

Pain flashed across Dare's eyes before he could pull down his mask of indifference. Guilt washed through Adam. He knew how sensitive Dare was about his failed marriage. About leaving Helen with that uncaring bitch of a mother. He'd stayed in the marriage longer than he should have, trying to make it work, until Ann had finally pulled the plug. And through it all, Dare had never abandoned Helen, even though she could be a huge pain in the ass, doing almost everything she could to drive him away. To prove that he was just like every other man who had been in her life.

His expression totally closed, Dare simply stared at Adam with his icy blue eyes.

"We'll just have to let Ash decide which of us she wants."

Ashley rang Dare's doorbell, her nerves frayed. The last time they'd spoken—the day he'd inundated her with flowers and told her he wanted a real relationship with her—they'd agreed to talk again today after she'd had a couple of days to think.

Dare opened the door and she found herself caught in his intense blue gaze, feeling outside her league. He was older than her, more experienced in life, and in total control of everything around him. The one exception was

Helen, but even there it was clear that she behaved that way on Dare's indulgence.

He smiled, his eyes glowing, and she felt . . . filled with sunshine. Like he considered her the most important thing in the world.

"Ashley," he said in his deep, smooth-as-silk baritone voice. "Come in."

He took her hand and drew her into the foyer, then closed the door. Before she could say anything she was in his arms gazing up at his heated midnight eyes.

"I'm so glad you're here," he said warmly. "I've missed you."

She found herself trembling as she saw the need glowing in his eyes and felt it building inside herself, sweeping away the nervousness about their discussion. He lowered his lips to hers and that first brush of flesh on flesh took her breath away. Then the pressure of his mouth increased and his tongue swept over her lips. She opened and he glided inside and stroked. She melted against him, glad for his strong arms around her as her knees threatened to buckle.

Good God, he'd never kissed her like this before.

He deepened the kiss and she clung to him, giving over her body to his masterful guidance.

When his lips parted from hers, she gazed at him, stunned.

"I thought we were going to talk."

He chuckled. "There's plenty of time for that later. Right now . . ." He dipped and she felt his arm behind her legs, then he swept her up. The world tilted and she felt herself gliding through the air as he carried her toward the bedroom. ". . . it's time for action."

A part of her wanted to protest. She shouldn't let this happen until she'd sorted out her feelings about the two of them. Until she'd chosen.

But she didn't want to choose. And Dare's lips nuzzling her ear as he strode down the hall made it too difficult to think. To resist what she wanted right here. Right now.

His lips grazed her neck and desire trembled through her.

She didn't want to worry about choosing one of them. Or hurting one of them. She just wanted to be lost in these delicious sensations.

He set her on the bed, then stepped back. She watched in fascination as he unbuttoned his shirt, slowly revealing the muscles beneath. He slipped it from his shoulders, then unzipped his pants and let them drop to the floor. He stepped toward her and her gaze locked on the growing bulge in his black briefs. She licked her lips, wanting to see his naked cock, thick and pulsing with need. Wanting to taste it.

She rested her hand on his rock-hard stomach and stroked downward, then over his thick shaft, feeling it twitch beneath the thin cotton. She pulled the top of his briefs forward, revealing his mushroom-shaped cockhead. Then lower, revealing more of his lengthening shaft. She wrapped her hand around it, loving the pulsing heat within her grip. She leaned forward and glided her lips over his cockhead, caressing it, then she opened wide and took him into her mouth. She sucked, pulsing her mouth around him.

He groaned softly. "Oh, God, Ash. I love it when you do that." He forked his fingers through her hair, sliding them through the strands.

She swirled her tongue over his tip, then glided deeper onto his cock, letting it fill her mouth more.

He coiled his hand in her hair and dragged her head backward, almost to the tip of his cock.

"As much as I love what you're doing, I had something else in mind."

He pulled her from his cock and back until she was gazing up at him, her head held firmly in place by his grip on her hair. He smiled, then dipped down to brush his mouth on hers.

"I want you to lie on the bed."

It wasn't a command, which surprised her. Wasn't he going to take control?

She lay back as he requested, watching him. He knelt in front of her and his fingers brushed against her chest as he unbuttoned her dress. When he finished the buttons to her waist, he drew back the soft floral fabric to reveal her dusty mauve bra beneath.

He smiled. "Very pretty." His finger traced along the scalloped lace edge of the cup, sending goose bumps dancing across her flesh.

He unfastened the rest of the buttons, then peeled aside the skirt. She lay there, her chest heaving, her body exposed to him in just her bra and skimpy matching panties. He tucked a finger under the top of her panties and drew them forward, just as she had with him, then peered inside. Her inner passage tingled as heat washed through her.

He smiled, then drew her panties down, slowly easing them past her hips. He glided his hand under her lower back and lifted so he could tug the panties downward, then he slid them down her legs and dropped them on the floor.

His hot gaze, locked on her intimate flesh, sent heated awareness through her. She felt wetness pooling between her legs and her nipples swelled against the lace. He rested his hands on either side of her folds, framing her between them.

"Your pussy is so damn sweet."

His thumbs stroked her thighs in small circles and she parted her legs automatically, aching for his touch. He chuckled in delight. Then his head dipped down. When his lips brushed her inner thigh, an inch from her tender flesh, she sighed.

His tongue glided over her skin, then he lifted his head and she felt a wash of air on her intimate flesh. His fingers brushed against her and she murmured her approval. He stroked along her folds, lightly, causing tremors of delight to ripple through her.

"You are so soft. And wet for me already." He lifted his head, gazing at her, his fingers hovering a breath above her. "Do you want me, Ash?"

She arched upward, but his fingers stayed out of reach.

"Yes," she breathed, just wanting to feel his touch again.

"I want you, too," he murmured. "You have no idea how much."

Then his mouth dropped and the exquisite feel of it on her sensitive opening filled her with joy. He covered her flesh and drew it into his mouth, suckling lightly. Then his tongue glided along the slick flesh in sure strokes. She slid her fingers through his thick waves of hair, wanting to pull him closer, but he took her hand, entwining his fingers with hers, and drew it aside.

He lifted his head and gazed at her, his face glistening. "I'm going to make you come, and I want to hear my name on your lips. Will you do that for me?"

Her eyes widened at his request—more because it was a request—and she nodded.

Then his mouth dropped again and he found that special place—the bud of flesh that became the center of her world when he touched it—and he suckled. She moaned at the pleasure pulsing within her. He licked and swirled over it, then suckled again.

"Oh, Dare. That's so good."

He chuckled against her, the warmth and vibration sending her pleasure higher. She arched and he drove his tongue inside her, stroking her moist channel. Then she felt his fingers glide inside her. His mouth moved to her clit again as he moved his fingers in and out in slow, gentle strokes.

Her breathing accelerated as he stroked and licked her. Her nerve endings quivered with pleasure, sending heat washing through her entire body. She pushed against his hand, wanting to grasp his head and pull it tight to her, but he held firm. When she gave up and relaxed, he stroked his fingers between hers, then along her palms and over the sensitive undersides of her wrists. Tingles danced along her skin.

Then he suckled again and she gasped.

His fingers moved faster inside her and she squirmed

beneath him, wanting more. Needing more. His tongue vibrated on her clit while his fingers thrust deeply in and out. Her whole body quivered, then shuddered as intense pleasure swelled inside her belly, then radiated outward.

"Oh, I'm so close."

She could feel him smile against her. His fingers seemed to dance inside her, stroking her passage as they moved deep in her body. Her insides tightened, coiling like a spring. His tongue lapped over her clit, then he suckled again.

Then her belly pulsed and she tightened her fingers around his.

"Oh, Dare. Yes."

Then it exploded in a sweet, effervescent fountain of joy.

He heard his name on her lips, a long reedy cry of pure bliss, as her body arched, thrusting against him.

His fingers kept filling her, and his mouth, so hot on her, stoked her expanding orgasm, urging it onward. Filling her with complete joy.

Her head spun and she laughed at the sheer ecstasy of it. She barely realized her hand was free as she stroked his hair, holding him tight to her, while his hands cupped her ass, his mouth working her like an expert.

Finally, she shattered completely, riding the wave he kept rising within her. She sucked in air, her throat hoarse from her continuous wails, then finally she fell limp to the bed.

After a few seconds, she opened her eyes and found him resting on his elbow beside her, grinning broadly.

"You seemed to enjoy that."

Laughter bubbled from her and she wrapped her arms around him and kissed him, tasting herself on his lips. His tongue glided inside her mouth and the passion of his kiss took her breath away.

Then he pressed her back and reached around her to unfasten her bra. He stripped it away, then his mouth found her nipple and he suckled.

"Oh, God, Dare." Then she whimpered.

He found her other nipple and licked and suckled until she was nearly in tears from the pleasure. He stood up in front of her and reached for her to rearrange her on the bed, but she wrapped her hand around his cock.

"No. I want to taste you first."

His gleaming eyes locked on her with searing heat. He nodded.

She opened around him, his bulbous cockhead filling her mouth. Then she glided downward. Oh, God, it felt so good having his rock-hard shaft between her lips. She squeezed, then drew back and sucked on his cockhead. She swirled her tongue around the ridge, then sucked again, loving his groan of pleasure. She cupped his balls and caressed them gently. Then she licked down his shaft and nuzzled her lips against the shaved sacs. When she took one inside her mouth, he groaned again. She caressed it with her tongue, pressing it to the roof of her mouth in a gentle wave of movement. He moaned, and his cock hardened even more.

"Enough, sweetheart."

His hands slid under her arms and he drew her upward. She managed a few kisses along his abs and his chest before he captured her lips and drilled his tongue into her, pulsing deep. Then she found herself on her back, sinking into the mattress, his body on top of her.

"God, I want you, baby. I want to be so deep inside you I might never find my way out."

"Oh, Dare. I want you, too. I want you inside me. Filling me. Making me complete."

He kissed her face. Butterfly kisses over her eyelids. His mouth covering hers. His tongue tangling with hers. She arched against him, loving the feel of his hard chest against her breasts. The sprinkling of coarse hair abrading her sensitized nipples.

His thick erection pressed against her belly, but she wanted it lower. Gliding over her moist flesh, then burrowing deep inside her.

He ground against her, continuing to kiss her. She arched, trying to leverage her body higher, so she could capture him inside her.

He laughed, then brushed her hair from her face, just gazing at her with a broad smile. "You're in such a hurry."

She slid her hand between them, then wrapped her fingers around his thick cock. It pulsed in her grip.

"You can't tell me you're not ready," she said.

He kissed her again, his persuasive lips moving on hers. "I'm always ready for you," he murmured. "But I could stay like this all day. Pressed against your soft, warm body."

She squeezed him and he groaned. Then he laughed. "Especially when you do that."

"God, Dare. Please, I need you."

His smile slipped away and his smoldering blue eyes gazed into hers with an intensity she found unnerving.

"And I need you."

She trembled at the tightly reined passion in his tone.

His body lifted from hers and he swept her hand away and grasped his cock. It glided over her slick opening and she widened her legs, inviting him in. He pulsed against her molten flesh, his cockhead barely dipping into her. She arched, wanting more, but he denied her. Giving her a brief taste of his hard flesh, drawing back, then dipping in a little again. He continued teasing her, giving her a mere inch at best, and she moaned in frustration.

Then he kissed the tip of her nose and . . . Oh, God, his thick shaft glided deep inside her. She swallowed him inside her body, her passage stretching around him. Accepting him.

She cried out at the exquisite pleasure.

"Ah, fuck, Ash. It's like I've died and gone to heaven."

He kissed her again. As he drew back, she cupped his hard ass, determined not to let him escape.

He pulled almost all the way out, her fingers tightening around him, then he glided forward again. Pleasure pummeled her senses.

"You like that?" he asked, his voice hoarse.

"Yes. You feel incredible inside me."

He drew back and glided deep again, taking her breath away. He nuzzled her ear as he sped up, his thrusts deep and steady. Making her head spin. Filling her with joy.

She surrendered to the rhythmic thrusts of his body, allowing him to carry her to a heavenly place of euphoric bliss.

"I . . . want . . . you . . . so . . . much." His words were punctuated by thrusts.

She quivered as he nuzzled her ear. There were so

many delightful sensations fluttering through her body and she was so close to the precipice.

"Ashley." His breath quivered against her ear just as she reached the pinnacle. "I love you."

She gasped, then her world exploded in an earth-shattering orgasm, blasting her to new heights of pleasure.

He continued to pump inside her, then drove deep, pinning her to the bed as he groaned his release.

She drew in deep breaths as ecstasy slowly faded, his big body over hers, his cock deep inside her still pulsing. His arms held the bulk of his weight but she felt trapped. He rolled onto his side and propped his head on his hand as he watched her.

She grasped the edge of the sheet and drew it tightly to her, feeling a little too exposed. Then she cleared her throat.

"You love me?" she asked.

He smiled, his eyes twinkling.

"Why did you say that?" she stammered. She didn't know why she was so thrown off. She loved him. Him loving her should bring her joy, not make her nervous as a cat.

"Because it's true. And I thought you'd want to hear the words."

"But . . . I'm in love with Adam." Then she bit her lip, wishing she could suck back the words.

His eyebrow arched. "Then why are you here?"

Her eyes widened and her breath caught in her throat. Oh, God, he thought the worst of her. She tried to scramble from the bed but he caught her arm.

"Ash, I'm not accusing you of cheating on him. I know

you've been straight with him. And you came here to talk so we could figure things out." He pulled her into his arms and held her close. "I just meant that you're here because you love me, too. Now we have to figure out what to do about it."

"You make it sound like there is a solution." She gazed at him hopefully.

"There's the obvious one . . . that you choose between us. But maybe there's a solution that might lead to all of us being happy."

Joy swirled through her, fluttering like a long silk scarf in a breeze.

Ashley pulled the robe around her and tied the sash at her waist, then opened the bathroom door. Dare had refused to tell her more, suggesting they continue the conversation over dinner. She'd taken a shower and dried her hair, now she smiled as she looked forward to sitting in his elegant but cozy dining room and gazing at him across a candlelit table.

She walked into the living room and saw he was sitting on the couch. And there was no hint of dinner cooking.

He stood up and smiled as he stepped toward her. "You look wonderful in my robe."

He pulled her close and kissed her. His tangy, masculine cologne reminded her of their bodies tangled together and desire blazed through her.

She stroked his chest and smiled. "Maybe we should save dinner and our conversation until later." As much as she wanted to hear what he had to say, right now she wanted him more.

He chuckled and kissed the tip of her nose. "I would love to, but unfortunately both dinner and our conversation will have to wait. Something came up and I have to leave."

Disappointment washed through her. And a niggling thought that it was probably Helen who was interrupting them.

She unfastened the sash on her robe and let it fall open, then she took his hand and slid it under the fabric to rest on her naked stomach.

"Are you sure I can't entice you?"

"Ash, I really have to . . ."

But she slid his hand to her breast and cupped it over her soft flesh. His sentence faded to a groan. He tightened his hand around her and her nipple hardened, pushing into his palm.

"You're a hard woman to bargain with because you know exactly what I want."

She pushed herself on her tiptoes and nuzzled under his chin, dragging her teeth over the whisker-roughened flesh. "So you'll stay?" she asked in her deepest, most seductive voice.

"I want to, baby. I do." But he drew his hand from her breast, then pulled her robe together and retied her sash, tugging it snugly closed. "But I really have to go."

She frowned as he walked across the room.

"I'll wait until you get dressed so I can see you out."

She turned, dejected, and went back to the bedroom, then returned moments later dressed and ready to go.

"So is it business? Or Helen?"

His eyebrow arched. "Does it matter?"

She followed him to the door.

"She just seems to take advantage of your good nature."

"My good nature? Most people think of me as controlling and hard to get along with."

She grinned. "They don't know you like I do."

"I would think you'd believe that more than anyone." He leaned in close and brushed his lips against her temple, sending tingles dancing down her spine. "At least the controlling part."

She ran her hand down his chest. "Well, I do love that about you."

He tipped up her chin and kissed her, his lips warm and enticing.

"But with Helen, you don't seem to take control enough."

He drew back and sighed. "Helen has problems. I know it seems like I'm too lenient with her, but she needs a special level of understanding."

"You know she's not a teenager anymore. But that's how she acts. She just seems to want attention, and it seems she'll do anything to get it."

How did she tell him his stepdaughter was a spoiled brat?

"Look, there are things you don't know. Let's just leave it at that for now."

They reached the door and he turned to face her, resting his hands on her shoulders, then gliding down her arms. "Now that we're in a relationship I know we need to talk about this, but I can't right now. I have to go." He leaned in and kissed her. His mouth was warm and persuasive, and he wrapped his arms around her, holding her close. Her heart fluttered in excitement.

Then he eased back, his deep blue eyes reflecting her own need.

"I'll call you later."

Ashley sank onto her couch and dialed Jessica's number.

"Hey, I was just going to call you," Jessica said when she answered.

"Yeah? Well, I just got home from Dare's." Her voice sounded morose, but she couldn't help it. She tugged at the tassel on the corner of the pillow beside her. "We were supposed to spend the evening together, but he got called away." She leaned back and stared out the window at the darkening sky. "I assume it was because of Helen. He always puts Helen first." She frowned, her heart aching at the feeling of rejection. "He'll probably always do that."

"Did he tell you he was going to see Helen?"

"No, but I asked him and he didn't say he wasn't."

"Well, I don't think he left this time because Helen called."

Ashley tightened her hand around the phone. "Why do you say that?"

"Because Helen's here with me. That's why I was going to call you. I think you should meet us for a drink. She has something to tell you that I think you should hear."

Ashley's stomach clenched as she pulled open the door to the lounge where Jessica had told her to meet them. It was very much Helen's taste. Trendy, upscale. And loud. The thrumming music pulsed through her as she walked past the dance floor to the back where Jessica had told her they'd be. Once she got there, she spotted Jessica waving at her.

"You're kidding," Ashley said as she sat in the small, curved booth, Jessica across from her and Helen around to the left. "It's a bit loud here to talk."

Leave it to Helen to suggest a place like this. It was better suited to hooking up than it was for conversation.

But she realized the volume wasn't so bad once she'd sat down in the booth.

"It's fine." Helen sipped from the straw in her tall, ice-filled drink.

Jessica gestured to a pitcher on the table. "I got sangria. Thought you'd like that."

"Sure," Ashley said.

Jessica tipped the pitcher, ice cubes tinkling against the sides of the empty stemmed glass as she filled it, then pushed it toward Ashley.

Ashley locked gazes with Jessica as she sipped, wondering where this was going.

"So you were at my dad's house tonight?" Helen asked.

"You already know that, Helen. Why did you want to talk to me?" Ashley asked.

Helen swirled her straw in her glass, sending the ice in circles, tinkling against the sides.

"I wanted to warn you about Adam Rawlins."

Ashley's eyes narrowed. "What about him?"

"I know you're seeing him, too. And as much as I'd rather you be with him than with my dad—"

"Your stepdad," Ashley corrected.

"Whatever. But as much as I don't want you seeing

Dare . . ." Helen frowned. "We were friends and I think you should know . . ."

Ashley glanced at Jessica and she shrugged.

"Know what?"

"You shouldn't trust him." Helen's hand tightened so hard around her glass, her knuckles turning white, that Ashley was surprised the glass didn't shatter. "He'll hurt you."

Ashley sucked in a breath. "Helen, I don't know why you walked away from our friendship years ago, or why you seem to want to strike out at me, but—"

Helen grasped her arm and leaned close. "No. You don't understand."

The intensity in Helen's eyes caught Ashley off guard.

"You need to listen. Adam . . . He . . ." Helen bit her lip, then let go of her tight hold on Ashley. "He was the cause of my mom and Dare's divorce."

Ashley didn't know what story she expected Helen to spin, but this certainly wasn't it.

"Adam? How could he possibly have anything to do with that?"

Helen took a deep sip of her drink, then leaned back against the padded bench.

"He and Dare were involved."

"What are you talking about?" Ashley demanded.

"He and my dad were lovers. When my mom found out, she left him."

Adam glanced up from his computer to see Ashley standing in the doorway to his office. The sight of her, looking so lovely in a slim-fitting blue dress that showcased her lovely figure, sent his heart pumping.

"What can I do for you?" he asked.

"Do you have a minute? You look busy."

"Always for you." He gestured to his chair.

Ashley stepped into his office and then closed the door behind her. He couldn't read her expression as she walked across the office and sat down.

"What's up?"

"I had a conversation with Helen yesterday."

"Really? I'm surprised. I didn't think you'd even agree to be in the same room with her."

"Yeah, she's not my favorite person right now, but Jessica convinced me to talk to her."

Adam closed his laptop and leaned back in his chair. "And what did she have to say?"

"Well . . ." Ashley fiddled with her hands.

He waited, giving her time to get it out.

Ashley's gaze locked on his. "She said that you were the cause of the divorce between her mother and Dare."

He frowned. "And why would she say that?"

"She said that . . . well, that you and Dare had a relationship."

"I worked for him as an intern."

"Helen said it was more than that. She said the two of you were lovers."

Crap. Would Ashley have the same closed-minded attitude that Ann had?

"I don't doubt that she's willing to lie to get what she wants," Ashley continued. "But in this case . . . she knows

I'm involved with you, and that helps her in her goal to push me and Dare apart . . . so her telling me something she thinks will push me away from you doesn't seem to make sense."

"So you believe her?"

"I don't know what to believe. That's why I came to talk to you."

"So what bothers you more? The idea that I had a sexual relationship with Dare, or that I broke up a marriage?"

"The idea of you and Dare being involved is . . . well, surprising. I never thought of you as being attracted to men. And I know you've always wanted to get married one day and have kids. Though I guess two men can do that with adoption and all—"

"Ash, you're babbling."

She sighed. "I know. I'm sorry. Okay, I think the idea of you loving who you love because of who they are, not based on what gender they are . . . not being afraid of what people think . . . that's a wonderful thing." She gazed at him. "But the thought of you cheating with someone who's married . . ." She shook her head. "I find that hard to believe."

"Good, because that part's not true."

"But the other part . . . about you and Dare . . . is true?"

He watched her. "Yes, it is."

She nodded. "Why would Helen tell me that you broke up their marriage?"

"Unfortunately, because she actually believes it."

"Why would she believe that?"

He stood up and started to pace. This was going to be tricky.

"You've got to understand that Helen took the divorce really badly. She never knew her real father because he abandoned her mother when she got pregnant. They were never married."

"I know that. She told me when we were younger."

"Her mother married two times before meeting Dare. Dare provided the only stability Helen had ever known and when she saw that marriage crumbling . . ." He stopped pacing and leaned against his desk, facing her. "I really can't say any more because Dare told me things in confidence . . . just that Helen was a mess."

"But why does she blame you?"

His stomach twisted. "I really wish I could answer your questions, but . . ." He shook his head. "I can't. You really need to talk to Dare."

"So now I have to go have this awkward conversation with Dare."

"You find it uncomfortable talking about Dare and I having had sex together?"

"You've both kept it hidden for all these years, so I assume it's uncomfortable for both of you, too. It is a little weird that you've been with each other and now you're both in love with me." She gazed at him with wide eyes. "Were you two in love?"

"Ashley, I really don't want to talk about this."

She frowned. "Sorry." She stood up. "I'll let you get back to work." She headed to the door, but when she reached for the doorknob, she hesitated, then turned back toward him. She tipped her head. "You know, Dare told

me he thought there was a solution to our relationship . . .
one where no one gets hurt. I didn't know about you and
him in the past, but now that I do, I wonder . . . Do you
think that maybe he's going to suggest that all three of us
have a relationship together?"

That sounded like something Dare might suggest. And
with Ashley's willingness to try new things, proven by her
embracing being Dare's submissive . . . and, God, by the
hopeful light shining in her eyes right now . . . His groin
tightened at the thought of Ashley, naked and eager,
standing between him and Dare. Of his lips on Ash. Of
Dare's lips on him. All three of their bodies moving together.

Oh, God, the thought turned him on so much. But it
also caused his heart to ache.

He turned and walked back to his chair and sat down,
the desk hiding his erection.

"Maybe, but it would never work."

"I know it's unconventional, but—"

"I don't mean that. I mean because I could never be
with him again." He shook his head, pain flashing through
him. "It was far too difficult the first time it ended. I don't
intend to go through that again."

Dare stepped out of his meeting, happy to have the papers
signed with the innovative owner of the high-tech start-up
to buy out his company, and to have him stay on to manage development of the new product here in town. The
chip he'd developed to allow small devices to quadruple
the memory they could hold was ingenious and would rev-
olutionize the capabilities of all mobile devices. He got
on the elevator and the doors closed behind him.

Now that he had successfully concluded his business here in Autumn's Ridge, he had no reason to stay.

Except to be with Ashley.

That was a pretty big reason.

He wasn't sure how to proceed with her. He didn't want her to pick Adam over him just because of proximity. He could return every weekend to see her, but that wasn't ideal for either of them. Especially with the current situation where she saw Adam every day . . . ran with him regularly . . . and she'd probably keep seeing him for their weekly movie night. Unless he forbade her, which he was sure would not go over well.

What he really wanted—what he'd been going to suggest to her—was that they try it with the three of them, but that was a pretty big leap and he wasn't sure he could convince her. He was actually relieved he'd been called away on business before he'd recommended it.

What he had to do was convince her to choose him over Adam. He was sure he could do it but . . . his chest tightened . . . he hated knowing that would cause Adam pain. But Dare had to look out for his own happiness, too.

And Ashley's.

He walked across the lobby toward the glass doors. It was a beautiful sunny day outside. He wondered what Ash was doing right now.

He pulled his cell phone from his pocket and glanced at his texts. There was one from Ashley.

Can we talk? I finish work at 5.

He glanced at the time display. It was almost five now.

He left the building and his driver opened the door of

the town car for him. He slid into the backseat, then tapped
in a return text.

Pick you up in 5 min?

The magazine was about eight blocks from here. He
gave the driver the address.

As soon as Ashley got the text from Dare, she closed up her
e-mail and grabbed her purse from her desk drawer. When
she hadn't heard back from him, she didn't think they'd
connect this evening, but he must have been in a meeting.

"You're leaving early tonight."

Adam's voice startled her. She hadn't seen him walking by.

"It's after five," she said defensively.

He laughed. "I wasn't complaining. You've been staying
late a lot these days. I think it's good that you're getting
away on time for a change. Got a hot date?"

"I'm going to talk to Dare tonight. About what we
were discussing yesterday."

Adam nodded. "I see. Well, I'd say have a good time,
but . . ." He shrugged.

The flickering conflict in his eyes was almost comi-
cal. She could tell he wanted to convince her not to go,
but he knew she had to talk to Dare to find the answers to
the questions raised yesterday. Of course, he was afraid
she'd go back to Dare's place and that they'd have sex.
Adam probably wanted to drag her into his arms and kiss
her senseless so that he could convince her to go home
with him instead. Or maybe he wanted to drag her into
his office and make good on his suggestion of bending her
over his desk and taking her.

The thought sent desire shimmering through her. She missed Adam and wanted to be in his arms again.

But Dare was probably waiting for her downstairs right now.

"I'm sorry, I have to go." She picked up her purse and hurried to the stairs, not wanting to wait for the elevator. It was only five floors down.

When she reached the lobby, she hurried across the marble floor toward the entrance, a little winded. She stepped out onto the sidewalk and drew in a deep breath of the warm fresh air.

Dare stood leaning against a shiny black car, looking devastatingly handsome in a charcoal business suit, tailored to perfection. She hadn't seen him in a suit before and the effect was . . . wow!

He opened the door for her and she slid into the car. He climbed in beside her, then the car moved away from the curb and into the traffic.

"Thanks for picking me up."

She'd barely finished the word when she was in his arms, his lips moving on hers, his tongue gliding into her mouth, claiming her completely. She melted against him, giving herself over to his powerful masculine authority.

Her desire for him surged and she fully expected him to press her down on the seat and take her right here.

Her heart pounded. She wanted him to.

He released her lips and smiled. "My pleasure. I'm happy to pick you up anytime."

"Um . . . thanks. Where are we going?"

"Back to my place."

She eased away from him. "Uh, no. I was hoping we could go out for a drink."

He smiled. "We can have a drink at my place."

"No, I'd rather go out." She did not want to be alone with him. Talking would turn into something more intimate and she didn't want that. Not until she figured out a few things.

"All right." He told the driver to take them to a bar she hadn't heard of before. They arrived about five minutes later.

Dare opened the door and she stepped into the classy bar. The walls were a rich burgundy with the bar and tables in glossy dark cherry wood. The chairs around the tables were upholstered with armrests and looked really comfortable. The hostess guided them to a table by the window, overlooking a garden with a lovely view of rich pink peonies and tall purple-and-yellow-bearded irises in full bloom.

"Nice place." Ashley sat in the chair Dare pulled out for her.

Dare sat down and ordered a bottle of champagne.

"Champagne?"

He smiled. "I closed a business deal today. I want to celebrate."

"Oh, does that mean you've finished what you came here for?" she asked.

"Ash, I'm not going to suddenly leave, I promise you that."

"But you will leave."

He rested his hand on hers, sending warmth washing up her arm and through her entire body. "We'll figure it out, Ash. Together. I know we can make something work."

The waitress appeared with the bottle and popped the cork, then poured the bubbly liquid into tall flutes and placed one in front of each of them. She put the bottle in an ice bucket by the table, then left.

"To us." He clinked his glass against hers.

"To your business deal." She sipped her wine. It was a delicate, delightful flavor. Like nothing she'd ever tasted before. Of course, it was probably very expensive.

"Dare, I don't want to ruin your celebration, but I have something to talk to you about."

He frowned. "It sounds like something I don't want to hear. If you've decided on Adam over me, I'll warn you, I'm not going to give up."

"It's not that. It's just . . . Helen came to talk to me about something and I just wanted to understand some things."

"Like what?"

"She told me that you and Adam . . . well, that you had a relationship in the past. I've already talked to Adam about this and he admitted that the two of you had an intimate relationship."

It was like a dark cloud passed over his face. The warmth of a moment ago disappeared behind a shield, his blue eyes guarded.

"Is that a problem for you?"

The chill in his voice threw her off guard and she hesitated.

"Because it was for Ann," he continued.

"But . . . Adam told me he and you didn't get involved

until after you decided to divorce. Are you saying that your relationship with Adam *was* what caused the marriage to end?" Her insides coiled at the thought Adam had lied to her.

"What? No, of course not." Then he sighed. "That's what Helen told you." He sipped his wine. "She won't let go of that. I've tried to straighten her out, but she just won't believe it."

"Then what did you mean about it being a problem for Ann?"

He sighed deeply. "Adam wasn't the first man I've been with." He pinned her with his gaze. "But not while I was married. I was never unfaithful."

She nodded.

"Ann found out and . . ." He stared into his flute while he swirled the liquid around. "Let's just say she's not very open-minded. She was disgusted by the discovery and said she would not stay married to a pervert. When she told Helen why she was divorcing me, Helen got the idea it was because I was cheating, not because of her mother's small-mindedness. When Helen found out about Adam and me, she just assumed it was his fault. I think it was because she needed someone to blame."

"I don't understand. How did it even start?"

"Adam worked for me as an intern. Since Helen asked me to find him the position, I interacted with him as much as I could to ensure he was getting what he needed to further his education. Then when things started going wrong with Ann and me, Helen started acting up. One night she let it slip that she was having sex with Adam."

Shock jolted through Ashley. "Oh, my God, Adam and Helen?" Her heart pounded, but Dare waved his hand.

"No. It turns out she was just yanking my chain. I confronted Adam about it and he told me, in as gentlemanly a way as he could, that Helen had thrown herself at him, but he'd turned her down. I'd suspected she'd been drinking and Adam reluctantly admitted it, not wanting to get Helen in trouble, but realizing that Helen had a problem and that I should know."

Jessica had told her about Helen drinking in school and now she was hearing this.

"How did that turn into a relationship?"

"Adam's a good listener. When I found out he knew about Helen's problem, I opened up to him." He raked his hand through his hair. "It was a tough time. I was going through this horrendous divorce, Helen was taking it hard—started drinking too much, getting into trouble. I couldn't tell anyone else what was going on. I didn't want people knowing about Helen's problem, hoping that I could get her straightened out and back to school, but in the end, it got so bad, I had to put her into rehab. That's why she didn't go to college."

She took his hand. "I knew it was hard on Helen, but I hadn't realized how much it messed her up. Or how difficult it was for you."

The waitress returned and refilled their glasses. Ashley took a sip, watching Dare as he stared at his glass.

She sucked in a breath, not wanting to drag him through more emotional turmoil, but needing to find out the answer that was key to them all moving forward.

"You know that it really hurt Adam when you left to move to New York. Why did you end it with him?"

"Fuck, Ash, I never wanted to hurt him. But what I had with Adam . . ." He gazed at her, his eyes begging her to understand. "It happened too fast, and at a time in my life where I couldn't really start a relationship. He thought we could make it work. I couldn't convince him otherwise." His hand curled into a fist. "Finally, I had to walk away."

"Abandoning him."

"What else could I have done?" His jaw twitched. "I tried to make him understand. He wanted to keep trying to make it work, but all I wanted was to be as far away from this town, and all the pain it represented, as I could get."

"So why didn't you get in touch with him later? Once your life settled down? I take it you weren't in love with him."

The troubled look on Dare's face shocked her.

Oh, God, it looked like . . .

Was Dare still in love with Adam?

Her heart skipped a beat. And if so, did she even fit in the picture? Could both Adam and Dare's feelings for her pale in comparison to what they felt for each other?

"I didn't try to start up a relationship with him again later for his own good. Once I had time to think about it, I knew it was a bad idea. Adam has always wanted to get married. To have kids. I felt he would be happier meeting a woman and getting those things in a more traditional way than with me."

"You didn't want to be a father?"

His eyes filled with pain. "Why would I? Helen is a

handful, and I seem to be doing a lousy job. What kind of mess would I make with my own children?"

"So you don't want to have kids?"

He raked his hand through his hair. "Oh, fuck, Ash. Of course, you want to have kids, and with me . . ."

She rested her hand on his arm. "Dare, you're a wonderful father. You stand by Helen through far more than most people would. You're patient and loving with her." She shook her head. "Don't blame yourself for a problem that existed long before you showed up."

He nodded, but she was sure he didn't really accept her statement.

"As for you and Adam and me. I'm curious about what you were going to suggest the other night, when you said you had a solution that might work for all of us. Were you going to suggest that maybe the three of us . . . ?"

His glance jerked to hers. "Is that something you'd consider?"

"Right now, it's a question of convincing Adam, not me."

Ashley walked along the path to Dare's front door, Adam by her side. She could feel the tension emanating from him. It hadn't been easy to convince him to come here.

"Do you really think this is a good idea?" Adam asked as they approached the entrance.

"Please give him a chance."

"I'm here, aren't I?" he said through gritted teeth.

She pressed the doorbell. Sunlight glittered on the beveled glass of the door. She saw a shadowy shape approaching through the glass. Too tall to be Helen. Dare had promised Helen would be nowhere near the house tonight.

The door opened.

"Adam," Dare said.

Adam nodded acknowledgment as he followed Ashley into the foyer.

"Come into the living room. I've opened a bottle of wine." Dare led them to the living room and Adam sat down beside Ashley on the couch. Dare poured them each a glass of white wine, then sat across from them.

The three of them sipped their wine, silence hanging over the room.

"Thank you for coming over, Adam," Dare finally said, breaking the uncomfortable quiet.

"I came because Ashley asked me to."

"Yes, I think it's important you two talk about what happened in the past. To try and heal old wounds," Ashley said.

"What's the point?" Adam asked, flashing Dare an acidic glance. "What's done is done."

"The point is to move forward." She took Adam's hand and linked her fingers with his. "Don't you want to make it work between us?"

"I want to make it work with *you*. I don't want Dare to deign to be with me just to keep you."

"Damn it, Adam. It wouldn't be like that."

Ashley's gaze jerked to Dare. Anger and pain warred in his eyes as he stared at Adam.

"Adam, I'm sorry I hurt you. I really am. But you know it didn't make sense for us to continue our relationship."

"Yeah, I know. Because you were going through a tough time with the divorce and all." Adam's hand clenched into a fist. "But you wouldn't even consider trying again later."

Ashley watched the two of them, hearing the emotion edging their voices.

"I didn't want you waiting around for me, especially since I thought that I wasn't the best choice for you."

Adam stared at him. "What the hell are you saying?"

Dare leaned forward. "I'm saying I wanted you to meet a woman, fall in love, then start the family you've always wanted."

Adam drew in a deep breath, his gaze locking with Dare's.

"You and I could have had a family. There are a lot of options, including adoption."

"But I know you really want your own child. With your own genes."

Adam's gaze filled with a longing that took Ash's breath away.

"I wanted you more," he said simply.

Ash choked up at the pain and longing in Adam's voice. Oh, God, these two men were meant to be together. If only they could see it.

Even if that meant she couldn't have either of them, it was a sacrifice she knew she had to make.

Pain slashed across Dare's face. "I'm sorry, Adam. I . . . just tried to do what's right."

"That's the problem, isn't it? You're always deciding for other people what they need. What's best for them. That's great in the bedroom. You are an exceptional Dom.

But that's where it should end. You decided for me, and you did it again with Ash. You need to let other people make their own decisions. Decide what *you* want, then let us decide what we want. In the end, everyone will be happier."

Dare drew in a deep breath. "You're right. That's exactly what I should do." He gazed at Adam, his eyes gleaming. "What I want is you."

Ashley's heart sank. She had succeeded in getting the two men together, but where did that leave her?

But then Dare gazed her way. "And you. I want both of you. I want us to make it work together."

Her heart pounded in her chest. Could this really be happening? Could she really have a relationship with both these men?

Her gaze turned to Adam, as did Dare's. If Adam didn't want this . . . and she couldn't blame him . . . then this wonderful dream would die right here and now.

"What do you want, Adam?" Dare asked.

"I want to hear from Ashley first."

"I . . ." She glanced from one to the other. "I want the same thing. I love you both. I can't think of anything better than to share my life with the two of you."

Adam's eyes gave nothing away. Ash held her breath.

"Adam," Dare said, "I promise I won't walk away from you again. Or Ashley. You'll have to drive me away with a stick."

Adam's lips compressed. Then he let out a long breath. "I believe you. But if we move forward with this, how would it even work?"

Her heart soared at his words. He was going to say yes!

"Well, you and Ash could get married, just as you told me you wanted to do, and I could live with you."

They had talked about her? About Adam marrying her?

"Or you and Adam could get married," Ashley suggested, "and I'd be the live-in mother of your children," she ventured with a grin, loving the idea of them recapturing their lost love and flaunting it in front of the world.

"Or we don't worry about social conventions at all and just commit to one another," Adam suggested as he stood up and stepped toward Dare. Then he took Dare's hand and pulled him close.

Ashley was blown away by the heat in his eyes. Their lips met and Ash drew in a breath at the sheer magnetic attraction she felt between the two men. Dare's arms went around Adam and her body heated at the sight of the two of them locked in a passionate embrace.

She realized she should leave. The two of them could use some alone time to catch up. To discover each other again.

She stood up and started toward the door.

"Stop." Dare's authoritative tone stopped her in her tracks.

She turned to see the two of them watching her, Dare's arm around Adam's waist.

"Where do you think you're going?" Dare asked.

"I just thought—"

"Come here, Ash," Dare commanded.

She turned and walked toward them. Both of them watched her with heat in their eyes and she felt tingles dancing through her body in response.

Dare grasped her wrist and drew her close. "Were you trying to run away?"

"No, sir."

"I think she was," Adam said, stepping behind her.

Dare curled his hands around her hips and pulled her tight to his pelvis. She could feel him growing hard against her. Adam moved closer, placing his hands on her shoulders, then glided them down her arms. They were both so big and so masculine, sandwiching her between them.

"Maybe we need to restrain her so she can't escape," Adam suggested.

"Good idea." Dare took her wrist again and guided her down the hallway toward the special room. He opened the door and led her inside.

"Nice," Adam said, glancing around.

"Take off your dress," Dare commanded.

Instantly, she unbuttoned the front of her dress, conscious of both pairs of male eyes watching her intently. She slid the dress from her shoulders, then let it drop to the floor, leaving her standing there in her skimpy panties and bra. She leaned over to pick it up, but Dare stopped her by grasping her wrist.

"Leave it."

He led her across the room, then leaned her over a padded bench, which was just wide enough to brush the underside of her breasts when she was horizontal. Dare stretched her arm down the other side of the bench and wrapped a restraint around her wrist, then did the same with her other arm. He moved behind her and fastened her ankles with restraints, too, forcing her legs wide apart.

She could feel the two men behind her, looking at her. Her cheeks flushed.

"What a lovely view," Adam commented appreciatively.

"This is even better," Dare said as he tugged on the waistband of her panties, pulling the crotch tight against her folds and between her buttocks. Then he tucked the crotch to one side.

"Oh, yeah. Much better."

She could hear the smile in Adam's voice.

"What about this?" Adam asked and she felt a finger glide under the back of her bra and tug on the elastic.

"Take it off," Dare said.

The hook released and the bra slid down her arms, dangling around her bound wrists. Adam's big hand cupped one of her breasts and caressed it. Her nipple hardened in the warmth of his palm. It felt strange with the remains of what she wore in disarray, but also sexy.

"Now that she's undressed, I think you should be, too," Dare said to Adam.

The two of them had moved in front of her so she could see the flash in Adam's eyes.

"Is that an order?" Adam challenged.

Dare's eyes glittered. "Oh, most definitely."

Tingles danced through her as she watched Adam strip off his shirt, revealing his broad shoulders and washboard abs. Dare watched intently, too. Adam unbuckled his belt. The sound of his zipper pulling down seemed to echo through the room, then his jeans fell to the floor with a clunk. The outline of his very hard cock was clearly visible through his snug boxers.

Dare smiled. "Don't stop there."

Adam tucked his thumbs under the elastic of his boxers, then pushed them down. His impressive erection fell forward.

Dare's eyes darkened and he moved closer to Adam. Her breath caught when Dare wrapped his hand around Adam's cock and squeezed, then stroked him. Adam's eyes fell closed, clearly in rapture at Dare's touch. Then Dare pulled him close and kissed him. Passion flared between the two men as Dare's lips moved hungrily on Adam's. Adam groaned, wrapping his arms around Dare.

Ashley's insides ached in need. She wanted to be touched, too, but watching them was exciting beyond belief. Dare sank to his knees in front of Adam and stared at the big cock in his hand. Then he licked it, from base to tip, to Adam's murmur of approval.

Dare opened and took Adam in his mouth, then glided deep, taking Adam's whole impressive length down his throat.

"Oh, God, Dare, that feels so good." Adam's hand cupped Dare's head, his fingers gliding through Dare's dark waves.

Dare cupped Adam's balls, caressing them, as he glided along Adam's cock, until it almost slipped from his mouth, then he dove deep again. He moved on the big cock several times, then finally, his mouth slipped off. He lifted the big shaft, then licked Adam's balls, drawing one into his mouth.

Ashley ached at the erotic sight.

Then Dare stood up. "Now I want you to look at Ashley." He guided Adam behind Ash and she felt a tug on her panties again.

"What a beautiful ass," Dare said. "Now touch it."

Adam's fingers lightly stroked over her ass. Tingles danced through her. He cupped her with both hands and squeezed gently.

"What about that pussy?"

"It's beautiful," Adam answered.

"Have you seen her pussy before? Have you touched it?" Dare's finger glided along her ass, so close to her tender flesh.

"Yes."

"I want you to tell me if she's wet."

Oh, God, she was so wet.

Adam's finger brushed against her flesh, but Dare immediately pulled it away.

"No, use your cock."

Her insides fluttered in anticipation.

Something thick and hot pressed against her damp flesh, then glided along the length of her slit.

"Oh, yeah. She's soaking wet."

Dare laughed. "Good. Now go and push your cock into her mouth."

Adam appeared in front of her, his cock stiff and long, pointing straight at her. Adam wrapped his hand around his shaft then pressed the slick tip of him to her mouth. She opened and he guided his cockhead inside. She stretched her mouth around him until his cockhead was fully inside her mouth, then she sucked.

"Oh, baby, yeah."

Then she felt Dare stroking her inner thigh. She stiffened, waiting for his finger to glide over her slick flesh. When it didn't, she lifted her ass in encouragement. Instead of moving his fingers to her folds, he cupped her ass with both hands and widened the flesh. Then she felt his mouth brush against her.

She moaned around Adam's cockhead. Adam glided deeper into her mouth. Dare licked her slit, then his fingers found her clit. He teased it and she moaned. Adam drew back.

Dare's mouth left her and she whimpered.

"I think I'm distracting Ash from sucking you off." Dare stepped behind Adam and crouched down. His hand tucked under Adam's balls and he cupped them.

"Ash, now you can focus on making Adam happy. Give him the best blow job ever."

She glided deeper on his big shaft. She sucked, then swallowed, causing a deep suction that made him groan.

"Fuck, Ash. That's incredible."

She opened her throat, then glided forward, taking him incredibly deep. He drew back, then slid forward again. His fingers curled through her hair and he guided her. His cock moved in and out. She squeezed as he moved between her lips. He drew out, leaving just his cockhead in her mouth and she took the hint and sucked. Hard. Causing that deep suction again.

"Fuck, I'm so close."

"Take him all the way, Ash. Let me see him fill your mouth with come."

She sucked, pulsing her mouth around him. His fingers tightened around her scalp and he groaned. She could feel his cock swell, then he jerked forward, hot liquid erupting in her mouth.

She kept on sucking until the flow stopped, then

she lapped her tongue around his shaft. Slowly, he drew his cock from her mouth and she swallowed his salty seed.

"Fuck, that was so hot," Dare said, standing up.

Adam dropped to his knees. "Now let me do you."

Dare seemed to want to protest, probably wanting to stay in total charge, but as Adam pulled down his zipper, he stood frozen, need dancing in his eyes. Then Adam reached inside and drew out Dare's enormous cock. It pulsed within Adam's grip.

The two of them were inches in front of her, and she licked her lips at the thrilling sight of Adam pressing Dare's cock to his lips, then him opening around Dare's huge cockhead. Adam took the whole thing in his mouth and she stared longingly at the long shaft protruding from his mouth.

"It's so sexy watching the two of you," she said.

Adam glided his hand up and down Dare's thick shaft as he sucked on the cockhead.

"Take it deeper," Dare commanded.

Adam glided forward, taking half the length into his mouth.

"Fuck, yeah. All the way, man." Then he grabbed Adam's head and pulled it tight to his groin.

Ash didn't know how Adam managed it, but he had the entire column deep in his throat. Dare ground his hips against Adam's face, then began to pulse his pelvis. Forward and back, fucking Adam's mouth. Adam stared up at him with a rapt expression, clearly reveling in the big cock filling him.

"That . . . feels . . . so . . . fucking . . . good!" The last word Dare uttered on a jerk forward. Then he groaned and held Adam's face hard against him again as his own face contorted in pleasure.

Ash could just imagine Dare's cock bursting inside Adam's mouth in sweet release. She could see Adam's throat move as he swallowed.

Finally, Dare pulled back, his deflated cock slipping from Adam's mouth. When Adam stood up, his cock was at full arousal again.

Adam turned to her, then cupped her naked breast, his fingers toying with her sensitive nipple. Dare fondled her other breast, his big hand gliding over her soft skin. He leaned in and nuzzled her neck. Delight tingled along her nerve endings.

"Do you want Adam to fuck you now?" he murmured against her ear.

"Oh, yes. Please, sir."

Adam's hand glided from her breast then he walked behind her. Anticipation blossomed within her and her breaths came quickly. He stroked her ass, gently circling over her skin. Then he smacked, catching her off guard. She gasped.

His cockhead brushed her damp flesh and glided along the length of her slit.

"Ohhhh." She lifted her ass in invitation.

"She wants it bad," Adam observed.

"Do you, Ash? Do you want Adam to drive his cock deep inside you?"

"Yes. Please, Adam."

Suddenly, the hard column of flesh drove into her. Deep and hard. Filling her to the hilt.

She groaned at the exquisite invasion. Her body quivered with need, her canal gripping him tightly.

Then he slid away slowly, his thick shaft stroking her. Sending need quivering through her. Then he drove deep again.

"What's it like to have his big cock inside you?" Dare murmured against her ear.

But all she could do was moan softly. Adam drew back, slowly, torturing her, then slammed hard against her body again.

"Oh, yeah," she whimpered.

He drew back, then drove deep again. And again. Filling her with long, slow strokes. She moaned as pleasure swamped her senses. Then he switched to short, fast strokes. Her breathing accelerated. She squeezed around him, arching back against him to take him deeper.

"Are you close?" Dare asked.

She nodded.

Dare stood up and kissed along her back as Adam pumped into her. Dare's cock, which was growing hard again, brushed her face. She nuzzled against it, then wrapped her lips around the side and suckled as pleasure washed through her at Adam's deep thrusts.

She moaned against his hard flesh, then lapped her tongue against him as Adam rammed into her harder. Then joyful sensations burst inside her as rapture claimed her. She moaned, riding the wave of ecstasy.

"Come for us, baby," Dare said, crouching back down and watching her face raptly.

Adam drove hard, then groaned. His cock pulsed inside her and heat filled her passage.

"He's coming inside you, isn't he?" Dare asked, his deep blue eyes locked on hers.

While her whole body shuddered in release, she nodded.

After a few more seconds, Adam drew out of her body, leaving her feeling empty. But then another cock brushed against her. Her eyelids flew open and she realized Dare was no longer crouched in front of her. His big cock drove deep into her and she moaned. The lingering pleasure from the orgasm Adam gave her sparked again. Dare drove deep and hard, this thrusts jerking her against the bench. She cried out, delighting in his masterful control.

He fucked her like a jackhammer, fast and powerful. She gasped, then moaned as another orgasm exploded inside her.

He pulled out, then unfastened her ankle restraints as Adam freed her wrists. Dare helped her to her feet. As soon as Adam stepped close, she grabbed both their cocks and squeezed.

"Now I want both of you inside me at the same time," she uttered through clenched teeth, the need overwhelming her.

Their semi-erect cocks hardened within her hands.

"I want the two of you to fuck me so hard I lose consciousness."

Adam pulled her into his arms and sucked her lower lip into his mouth. "Fuck, baby, you are so hot."

But Dare's cock was a little slower at growing rigid, having just emptied inside her. She took his hand and pressed it to her wet pussy, then pushed his fingers inside along with hers. She stroked herself and he sucked in a deep breath.

"Who's going to fill my ass," she asked seductively, turning and pressing her ass against Dare's semi-erect cock. She ground against him, to his moan.

Adam moved closer, then pressed his cock to her moist opening. He teased it, then pushed inside. Dare pushed his cock, now hard as rock, against her anal opening. The pressure increased as his cockhead stretched her open. Adam found her clit with his fingers and stroked it. Electrical sensations shot through her. Dare's cock continued to push inside, stretching her uncomfortably wide, but Adam's teasing fingers distracted her. She moaned at the fluttering pleasure radiating from the sensitive nub as Dare's big cock invaded her ass.

His groin pressed against her ass and she realized he was all the way inside her. Adam pushed in the rest of the way, his body pushing her tighter against Dare. Then the two men kissed each other over her shoulder. She turned to watch them, reveling in their big cocks deep inside her. Their lips found hers, both of them kissing the sides of her mouth. She opened and their tongues glided inside her mouth. She met them, swirling back and forth to caress both of them.

Then Adam began to move, pulsing his cock inside her, the movement jostling Dare's cock inside her ass. Their mouths parted and Dare pushed forward, his cock stroking her sensitive back passage.

Adam drove deep. Both of them held her tight between them, their cocks fully immersed.

Then they moved together. Both pulling back, then

driving forward in unison. They coordinated their thrusts, filling her deeply . . . pulling back . . . thrusting deep again.

"Oh, God . . ." Her voice cracked, then she wailed as ecstasy erupted inside her like a geyser. Sudden and powerful. Catapulting her to ecstatic heights.

"Fuck, baby." Adam's face looked fierce as he drove into her.

Dare's big cock filled her from behind.

Her moans grew louder as intense pleasure blossomed within her. The sound of their groans drove it higher and higher. When she felt them erupting inside her, their big bodies jerked tight against her, she wailed her release.

The whole world seemed to shatter around her and she slumped between them.

"Fuck, did she actually lose consciousness?" Dare asked.

She giggled, still riding high on the blissful experience.

"Are you kidding? I didn't want to miss a second of that."

Adam chuckled and the two of them held her close. She'd never been so content in her life.

"Did you like that, Ash?" Dare murmured against her ear.

"Oh, yes, sir." She snuggled between their bodies. "All I can say is, more, please."

Dare woke up to the sound of soft murmurs beside him. He rolled over and saw Adam on top of Ash, her legs wide and wrapped around his waist. Dare blinked his eyes open wider, watching Adam's thick cock gliding in and out of her.

Adam stroked her hair from her face as he fucked her, their gazes locked together, love filling their eyes.

God, the sight of them made his heart melt. They were obviously so much in love. A part of him told him he was just in the way. That with the way he could see they were, he should just walk away and let them be together, just the two of them.

But he'd promised Adam he wouldn't do that kind of thing anymore. Make decisions for other people. Assuming he knew what made them happy.

Adam drove deep and Ash moaned softly. She glided her fingers through his hair as his lips nuzzled against her neck. Their pace quickened and their breathing accelerated.

"Oh, Adam. I'm going to come."

"Do it, baby. Right now."

She moaned, her eyelids fluttering closed. The ecstasy on her face made Dare ache inside.

"I'm . . . coming," she uttered on an exhale.

Adam drove deep and groaned. Fuck, he was coming inside her right now.

Dare watched the two of them, totally caught up in their pleasure. Then they stopped moving, Adam's body on top of hers while they both caught their breath. Finally, Adam rolled back with a sigh.

Ash turned her head toward Dare.

"Oh, you're awake." Then she smiled and rolled toward him. Before he knew it, she was sitting on his thighs, her hand around his rock-hard cock.

"Did you get turned on watching us?" she murmured against his ear.

"How could I not?" he responded, his voice raspy.

She laughed, deep and throaty. Then she pressed his cockhead against her slick slit and lowered herself on him.

Oh, God, heaven itself couldn't feel better than this. Being surrounded by her velvety softness took his breath away.

Then she moved on him. Lifting and lowering her body. His cock gliding deep into her heated passage, then sliding back, then swallowed deep again.

"Baby, I'm close already."

She smiled like a Cheshire cat. "Good. Because so am I." She sped up, taking him deep and fast. Then her breath caught and she moaned.

The sound of her orgasm . . . his cock deep in her slickness . . . was too much. His groin tightened and intense pleasure shot through him. He erupted inside her, groaning his release.

She sank onto him, resting her head against his shoulder. He tucked his arms around her and quickly realized she'd fallen asleep on top of him.

Adam moved in close and put his arm around Ash, his lips nuzzling against Dare's temple.

God, it didn't get better than this.

Ashley ran a brush through her hair, then applied her lipstick, a deep, dusty rose that complemented her skin tone. She was meeting Adam at Dare's tonight instead of Adam picking her up, since Adam needed to stay a little late at work to have things ready for a meeting on Monday morning.

As she walked down the hall to the living room, a

knock sounded on the door. Had Adam gotten off work early and come to pick her up after all?

She peered through the peephole. Shock vaulted through her at the sight of Helen on the other side. She debated not opening the door at all. She was in no mood for more of Helen's lies.

Helen knocked again.

Ashley opened the door.

"Hi, Ashley. May I come in?"

"Why are you here?" Ashley asked, not stepping aside.

"Look, I know. You're mad at me because of things I've said and done, but I really need to talk to you."

"All you do is lie to me, Helen. Why should I listen to you?"

"I didn't lie about Dare and Adam."

"But Adam wasn't the cause of the divorce."

"Says him. But I don't believe it."

Ashley could tell from Helen's face that it was the truth and she remembered Dare saying that Helen needed someone to blame. Without that, she might have to believe that she was the reason Dare had left. And every other man in her life. That's why she acted up, too. Because then if they left, she could blame it on the bad behavior rather than believing that she was basically unlovable. But deep inside, that was probably exactly what she believed.

Ashley sighed and stepped aside. Helen followed her into the apartment to the living room.

"Ash, I'm sorry," she said as she sank onto the couch. "I know I've said some things, and done some things"— she pursed her lips—"that must make you hate me. I've been confused and . . . well . . ."

To Ashley's complete surprise, tears welled in Helen's eyes.

"The thing is . . . I'm in trouble."

"Does this have to do with your drinking?"

Helen's eyes widened. "Dare told you about that?"

"You better get used to it. Dare and I are getting serious and he confides things to me." Ashley didn't want to tell her that they were in love, and she certainly wasn't going to tell her about Adam. She'd leave that to Dare to tell her in his own time and in his own way.

"Ash, I know you're probably not going to believe me—and I don't blame you—but . . ." Helen reached out and took her hand. "I'm scared and . . ." She gazed at Ashley with big dewy eyes. "I really need your help."

"Why my help? What's the problem?"

Helen bit her lip. "I'm pregnant."

Ashley's jaw dropped open.

"I was hoping that I could convince Dare to let me move in with him so he can take care of me and the baby, but that will never happen if Dare stays with you and . . . well, I know that the three of you are starting a relationship together. There's no way Dare will let me stay with all of you living together. I don't get along with Adam and . . . well, I've made you uncomfortable." She squeezed Ashley's hand. "I really need him and I'm afraid he'll send me away. And my mom won't have anything to do with me."

"Even if that happens, you can manage on your own. A lot of women these days—"

"No, that won't work. I can't get a job . . . you know how things are. Even if I can pick up a part-time job serving coffee or working in a store, I won't make enough to support me and the baby, especially having to pay for baby-sitting." Tears fell from Helen's eyes. "Please, Ash. I need your help. You have both Adam and Dare. If you just tell Dare that you choose Adam, then everything will work out for both of us. Dare will take care of me and the baby, and you'll still have Adam."

Ashley tugged her hand away. "No. You need talk to Dare and let him decide if he wants to help you and how, but it's not fair to Dare that I break up with him over this."

Helen stared at her, her gleaming blue eyes intense.

"Even if he's the father?"

Ashley felt numb as she drove to Dare's. She'd told Helen outright that she didn't believe that for a minute. He had even proven that when Helen had thrown herself at him in front of Ashley and he'd turned her down flat. But then, despite all Helen's previous lies and trickery, what Helen told her after that put enough doubt in Ashley's mind that now she wasn't sure.

She arrived at Dare's and parked beside Adam's car in the driveway. She walked up the front steps then rang the doorbell. Dare greeted her with a broad smile. But as soon as he saw her face, his smile faded.

"What's wrong?" he asked.

"We need to sit down. And I think strong drinks all around would be a good idea."

"Sounds ominous, but whatever it is can wait for this." He drew her close and kissed her, but as sweet and persuasive as his lips were, she stiffened.

He eased back, but still held her close, his penetrating

gaze locked with hers. "What's wrong, Ash?" he asked softly.

"We really need to talk."

His lips compressed. "No good conversation ever started with those words."

"What's going on out here?" Adam asked, standing in the foyer a few feet away.

Ashley's gaze lingered with Dare's, then she drew back and turned to Adam. "I was just telling Dare that we need to talk."

Dare didn't know what was going on, but the look in Ashley's eyes turned his blood cold. Whatever she wanted to talk about would be game changing. He could feel it in his bones.

She walked to Adam and Adam drew her close and kissed her. Dare could tell that she wasn't freezing up with Adam like she had with him. Fuck, so whatever was troubling her was definitely about him.

He followed the two of them into the living room. "Did you mean it about those drinks?" he asked as she sat on the couch beside Adam.

Her gaze caught on the open bottle of wine on the coffee table and she poured herself a glass. Dare and Adam already had full glasses.

"This will be fine." She sipped hers, then set the glass on the table.

Dare sat on the chair across from them.

"Just before I came here, Helen dropped by my apartment to talk."

Dare frowned. He didn't know what trouble Helen

had tried to stir up, but clearly it had had a profound effect on Ash.

"Well, she's afraid to tell you this, but . . . she needs help."

"She's needed help for a long time." He shook his head in confusion. "Why would she go to you about it?"

"To be honest, she came to me to ask me to break up with you."

"You're not going to listen to her, are you? You know she'll do anything to get attention from me. She's insecure and sees you as a threat to her relationship with me."

"I know. And I was ready to assume anything she said was a lie, but . . ." She locked her gaze with his. "Dare, she's pregnant."

The announcement took him totally by surprise.

"How do you know she's telling the truth?" Dare asked.

"I could feel her fear. She doesn't think she can do this on her own and she's afraid you won't be there for her. Especially when she tells you that . . . you're the father."

Shock spiked through Dare, striking him speechless.

"What the fuck?" Adam's glance bolted to Dare.

"Ash, you've got to know she's lying. You can't believe I'd do that."

"I know. Not on purpose, but . . . You remember that time I left in the middle of the night? She said she heard me go and slipped into your room a little while later, after you'd fallen asleep. She said that you thought it was me coming back in and . . ."

Horror shot through him as he remembered waking up with a feminine body snuggled against him.

"Oh, fuck. But . . . how . . ." He raked his hand through his hair. "When I woke up . . ." He snarled. "God damn it."

She'd been so soft and warm, and he'd assumed she was Ash. His body had done what was natural and hardened with need. Something had niggled at his brain that Ash shouldn't still be there, but his hazy brain had decided she'd come back. Then he'd fallen asleep again. In the morning, when Ash wasn't in his arms, he'd assumed he'd been dreaming.

"You mean, this could have really happened?" Adam asked.

"Fuck, I didn't . . . I mean, there's no way I could have . . ."

Ash rested her hand on Dare's arm. "Can you be absolutely sure? If you thought it was me . . ."

Could he have done something when she climbed into bed with him? While he was half asleep?

"No, it can't be true. It can't." But doubt spiked through him.

"If you did, it wasn't your fault," Adam said, understanding in his warm brown eyes. "She tricked you."

But even the thought that he could have done that with Helen . . . his own stepdaughter . . . made him feel ill.

Ashley got up and sat beside him on the couch. She took his hand and just held it. Adam moved to his other side and took his other hand. The comfort of these two special people beside him was his anchor. With them by his side, he could get through anything.

"Whatever you need to do, we'll support you," Adam said.

Dare shook his head, determination spiking through him. "Even if it is true, I won't leave you." He squeezed their hands. "Either of you. What the three of us have is special. The love we share is . . ." His chest compressed. "I can't lose that."

But he couldn't abandon Helen either. Even though what she had done was despicable . . . if she was carrying his baby . . .

Dare watched as Helen sat on the couch, looking properly contrite.

"So Ash told you," she said.

"Of course she told me."

"I'm sorry. I know I should have told you myself, but—"

"Told me?" he flared. "You shouldn't have fucking done what you did? What the fuck were you thinking? "

Her eyes widened and she stared at her hands folded in her lap.

"I know that I shouldn't have—"

"Do you?" he glared at her. He could see that her hands were trembling and she wouldn't look at him.

He let the silence simmer around them. Let it sink in to her exactly how much trouble she was in with him.

"I . . ." She shifted under his acidic stare. "I'd been drinking and—"

"Do you think that makes it okay?" he demanded.

"No." Tears rolled down her cheeks but he steeled himself to her discomfort. "I just . . ." She bit her lip, clearly reading from his expression that she was getting nowhere.

He sucked in a calming breath. "At first I tried to convince myself that it hadn't really happened. That you were just lying to . . . I don't know, I guess to trap me into taking care of you forever. But then I really thought about what happened that night. And . . ." His hand clenched into a fist. "God damn it, the very thought of what you did sickens me. I have been nothing but patient with you, but, fuck . . ." He slammed his fist on the table, sending vibrations through the room. "This is too much."

"I'm so sorry. Just . . . sometimes I feel so alone and scared . . . and you're the only one who's ever cared about me. I'm always so afraid that you'll walk away and—"

"All you've accomplished is to succeed in driving me away. As of now, you're out of my life."

She covered her face with her hands, sobbing. "Please, I know I have a problem. I'll do anything you want. Please, don't do this."

He stared at her, considering.

"You'll go into rehab again."

"Yes, of course." She stared at him, her eyes hopeful. "Anything."

He compressed his lips, letting the silence continue.

"What about the baby?" she finally asked.

He sighed. "The only responsible thing for you to do is put it up for adoption.

Ashley waited anxiously as Dare opened his front door, then she stepped into the foyer, Dare and Adam behind her. Dare had taken the three of them out to a nice dinner, but had refused to talk about his conversation with Helen until they returned to the house. She walked into the living room and sat on the couch, her stomach fluttering. Dare sat down beside her.

"So how did it go with Helen?" Adam asked as he sat down on the other side of Dare.

Dare sighed. "She'd been drinking and she did it to try and keep me in her life."

"That girl is truly screwed up," Adam said.

Dare nodded. "At least she's agreed to go into rehab again."

"Thank heavens," Ashley said.

A heavy silence hung between them, until finally Adam said, "So you're going to be a father."

Ashley's stomach clenched. Since Dare was the father, would he stick by Helen, even after what she'd done? Would he . . . could he even consider actually moving Helen in with him?

Dare pursed his lips. "Well, not really."

Ashley rested her hand on Dare's. "What do you mean?"

"She's putting the baby up for adoption." Dare's expression was strained. "She still has a lot of issues to work out and, especially given her drinking problem, it seemed the best choice."

Ashley curled her fingers around his hand. "Did she want to keep it?"

Had Dare talked her into adoption? Ashley couldn't imagine giving up a baby if she were pregnant. But as Dare said, with Helen's issues, it probably was for the best. But that didn't mean she would be happy about it.

"At first. But more because her father walked out on her and her mother and she didn't want to do the same. I explained that with adoption, the baby would go to a family that really wanted it. In the end, Helen's main concern is that the baby have a good home. It'll be hard on her, but it's for the best."

"It'll be hard on you, too, won't it?" Ashley asked, gazing into his sad blue eyes.

"It'll be hard to watch her go through the pregnancy, then have to give up the baby. To never see it again. And for the baby to never know her mother."

Or her father. But Dare probably didn't want to think about that.

"You know, the three of us want to have a baby," Adam said. "And we would be a great home."

Dare's gaze darted to Adam's. "What are you saying?"

"I'm saying that maybe the three of us could adopt the baby."

Ashley's eyes widened at the suggestion and her heart thumped loudly.

"But you want to have a baby that's yours," Dare said.

"I want a baby that's *ours*. And this baby is part of you."

Ashley bubbled with joy at the thought that . . . what they were talking about was them all having a baby together. Tears welled in her eyes and she blinked them back. If this happened, then . . . she was going to be a mother.

She gripped Dare's arm. "And if we adopt the baby, then Helen will be able to be a part of her life."

Dare's gaze turned to her. "You're on board, too, Ash?"

She smiled broadly. "I think it's a wonderful idea."

"What do you think, Dare?" Adam asked, eagerness lacing his words.

"I don't know, I . . ." Then Dare smiled broadly. "I think it's worth asking her."

When Dare returned to the room and sat between Ashley and Adam again, Ashley's stomach clenched at his dead-pan expression. None of them had wanted to wait so they'd decided Dare would phone Helen right away and ask her what she thought.

"So?" Adam prompted.

"Well . . ." Then a smile spread across Dare's face. "It seems we're going to be parents."

Adam laughed, a glorious sound full of joy. "Oh, my God. That's incredible."

Ashley gazed from one man to the other, the words and their meaning slowly sinking in.

"We're really doing this? We're adopting her baby?" Ashley asked.

"Yes, Ash." Dare took her in his arms and hugged her. "You're going to be a mother." He gazed down at her. "It's what you want, isn't it?"

She smiled so broadly, her cheeks hurt. "More than anything." She rested her hand on Dare's face. "Except when I have your baby. And Adam's."

Adam chuckled. "So we're going for three?"

She giggled, reaching for Adam's hand and holding it tight, while Dare still held her in his arms. "Or more."

Adam wrapped his arms around the two of them and they sat in the warmth of their embrace for several long moments. Ashley felt so much love around her it made her heart swell.

Finally, Dare drew back, then stood up, breaking the embrace.

"There is another matter we need to discuss. It's especially important now that we've made this momentous decision."

Ashley and Adam stared at him expectantly.

Dare knelt down on the floor in front of the couch and Ashley's heart beat faster. He took her hand in his. The feel of his big fingers enveloping hers sent warmth through her. He took Adam's hand, too.

"You both mean so much to me and I love you with all my heart. I can't imagine my life without the two of you in it. I may not be able to marry both of you, but I want us to spend the rest of our lives together."

"Oh, Dare." Tears sprang from Ashley's eyes and Adam wrapped his fingers tighter around Dare's hand.

"I'm hoping you'll both move in here, or we can buy a new place we all choose. I just want us to be together."

"What about New York?" Adam asked.

"I'm going to move back here. I've always loved Autumn's Ridge. That's why I moved here in the first place. I hated having to leave, but it was too hard after the divorce. Now . . . everyone I care about is here. Even Helen will be moving to town so she can be close to the baby."

Ashley reached for Adam's hand, searching his dark brown eyes. His eyes sparkled and he gave her a quick nod.

"Yes, Dare. Oh, yes," she said as she threw her arms around him. His lips found hers and he kissed her deeply.

When he released her, they both turned to Adam.

"Are you fucking kidding me? Of course the answer is yes."

Dare laughed, then embraced Adam. Their lips met with passion. Tears of joy trickled from Ashley's eyes and she swiped them away.

Dare stood up, a broad grin on his face, then he walked through the dining room and into the kitchen. He returned with champagne in a bucket of ice in one arm and three tall stemmed glasses in his hand. The bottle was frosty, so clearly he'd had it on ice before they'd arrived.

He set the bucket on the coffee table, then popped the cork. The frothy liquid bubbled up and he quickly poured it into the glasses.

Dare lifted his glass. "To a lifetime of happiness with the three of us together."

They all clinked glasses and Ashley sipped the delightfully bubbly wine.

Dare finished his glass, then topped everyone up.

He walked to the desk in the corner, then returned with a folder in his hand and sat on the chair across from them.

"We may not be able to marry legally, but if you both agree, I'd like to make it official."

He opened the folder and set a document in front of each of them.

"I want us all to be protected, so I had these drawn up."

Which probably meant he wanted to protect his wealth from any claim she or Adam might make based on a common-law arrangement, Ashley thought. But when she glanced through the agreement, it was quite the opposite. It talked more about the commitment they were making to each other than it did financial considerations.

Adam perused the document, then glanced at Dare. "This says that Ashley and I are entitled to an equal share of your assets."

"That's right. The three of us will own everything equally."

Adam flipped through the papers. "You do realize a prenup is supposed to protect *you*."

"I don't need protection. What I need is both of you in my life. And the money isn't the important thing in this document. It's the fact that it states our commitment to love and honor each other for the rest of our lives."

Adam's eyebrows arched. "Your lawyer must think you're crazy."

Dare chuckled. "True. But who gives a shit about that?"

Adam pulled a pen from his suit jacket and signed the three documents. Dare signed them, too, then handed Ash a pen and the three agreements. She signed them, then handed them back to Dare, feeling a little empty.

"Ash, you don't look happy," Adam observed. "Is there something wrong?"

"No, not at all." She smiled. "I'm very happy."

Dare reached out and took her hand. "Tell me what's wrong."

"It's nothing, it's just . . . Well, for all intents and purposes, after signing these, the three of us are married now."

"Isn't that what you want?" Dare asked.

"Of course, but . . ." She sighed, worried she'd sound shallow. "I just always dreamed of a wedding, with the long white dress, flowers, music. All of that." She squeezed

Dare's hand. "But the three of us being together . . . that's the important thing."

"Hell, Ash. There's no reason we can't have a wedding," Dare said with a big smile. "We'll exchange vows. And rings, too, if you want. We'll make up our own rules as we go."

"Really?" She couldn't believe how ridiculously happy his suggestion made her. Having a wedding would make it feel more real.

"Can we do it soon? Maybe next month?" Ash asked.

"That's not much time to plan a big wedding," Adam said.

"I don't need a big wedding. Just close friends and family. I just want us to stand up and proclaim to those closest to us that we love each other and will always be together."

Dare smiled. "Then next month it is."

"Great." Adam grinned. "Now that we've settled the wedding, what about the honeymoon?"

Ashley laughed, then climbed on Adam's lap facing him, her knees on either side of his thighs. "I think we should start right now."

Dare moved behind her and knelt on the floor. He cupped her breasts and nuzzled the base of her neck as Adam claimed her lips. Her nipples hardened in Dare's hands and her insides ached with need.

Adam tugged on the zipper of her dress, then Dare pulled it down the rest of the way. Adam peeled the dress from her shoulders and down to her waist. Her hard nipples pushed against the lacy bra. Adam tugged down the lace and took her nipple in his mouth. She sighed at the warmth around her. The bra loosened and Dare pushed down her straps and tugged the garment away. He slid in beside Adam and took her other nipple in his mouth. Her hands cupped their heads, holding them close to her chest as they suckled. Delightful sensations danced through her.

Adam gripped her waist and stood her up, then drew down her dress and panties. Both male gazes locked on her pussy. Dare leaned forward and licked her. She widened her legs, then Adam licked her, too. They alternated, their warm mouths teasing her with nibbles and licks. Then Adam sat her on the couch and pressed her knees apart. His face fell to her folds and he dug in, licking and suckling her clit until she moaned.

Dare kissed her mouth, his hand cupping her breast, his thumb stroking her hard nub. Dare drew back and watched her, their gazes locked as Adam sent her pleasure skyrocketing. She moaned, still locked onto Dare's mesmerizing gaze.

"I want to watch you while Adam makes you come," he murmured.

Adam's fingers slid into her and she arched. It felt so good.

Adam's tongue swirling over her . . . his fingers thrusting into her . . . Pleasure swelled and joy swept through her. She gasped, then moaned her release, lost in the deep blue of Dare's eyes.

The orgasm filled her being, expanding through her until she could barely breathe, wailing at the intensity of it.

Finally she slumped on the couch, sated.

It took a few moments for her to catch her breath, but

once she did she sat up and smiled at them. "Now I want to see Adam make you come," she said to Dare.

Dare stood up and unfastened his pants, then dropped them to the floor. Adam sat on the couch and reached for Dare's briefs, then pulled them down. Dare stepped out of them.

Adam wrapped his hand around Dare's long, hard cock and stroked it. Ashley watched, excitement coursing through her. Adam guided the big cock to his mouth and took it inside.

"That's nice, but I want to watch you make love to Dare."

"Really?" Dare's eyebrows arched. "It sounds like you want to be in charge."

She laughed. "No, just a request."

Dare leaned in and kissed her. "Are you sure? Because it could be sexy having you command your two men."

Excitement trilled through her at the thought. "Maybe I will. Maybe I'll chain you both to the wall and have my way with you. But right now I want to watch you together."

"Okay." Dare swept her into his arms and she squealed in surprise.

He carried her to the bedroom and laid her on the bed, Adam behind him. Dare shed his shirt, then prowled over her.

"But I thought—"

Dare interrupted her words with a kiss while Adam stripped off his clothes, then opened the drawer in the bedside table.

"You want to watch Adam make me come." Dare smiled. "You're going to get a close-up view."

Adam climbed on the bed behind Dare. He took her hand and pressed it to his rock-hard cock. She stroked it. Dare pressed his thick cock to her damp folds and glided the length of her.

"Oh, yeah," she moaned.

Adam drew her hand away and she realized he was holding a bottle of lubricant, which he applied to his erection.

Dare pushed forward, his cock gliding inside her. It filled her slowly, stretching as it moved deeper. Once he was fully inside, he kissed her.

"Now Adam is going to enter me."

"Oh, God." That was so hot.

She gazed at the mirror over the dresser to watch Adam press his slick cock to Dare's ass. Slowly, he pushed it inside. She watched fascinated as the bulbous head disappeared inside of Dare, the long shiny shaft following slowly. She turned to watch Dare's face. His eyelids were half closed and pleasure washed across his blue eyes.

"Does that feel good?" she asked him.

His cock twitched inside her, sending pleasure rippling through her.

"Fuck yeah."

Adam laughed, then he was tight against Dare's back. His lips captured Ashley's. As they kissed over Dare's shoulder, he nuzzled their cheeks. Adam released her mouth and captured Dare's for a moment. Then Dare kissed her.

"Now let's fuck," Adam said.

Dare drew back, his long cock gliding along her passage. Adam moved back, too. Then they both surged forward. She gasped as Dare's cock filled her. They drew back again, then both glided forward again.

Soon they were moving in a steady rhythm. As Dare's big cock filled her, she was intensely aware that Adam's cock was also filling Dare. The thought drove her need higher. They pumped into her again and again, Dare's face alight with pleasure.

She clung to Dare's shoulders as heat swelled through her. "Oh, God, I can't believe you're fucking me while Adam is fucking you."

"Every time I drive my cock forward," Adam said, his voice coarse with desire, "it's like I'm filling you, too."

"Oh, yes," she cried as he drove into her again.

Adam thrust faster and Dare groaned.

"Aw, fuck," Dare exhaled, then jerked into her. He moaned as liquid heat filled her. Adam groaned his release.

Blissful pleasure, sudden and intense, rocketed through her. She moaned, an orgasm washing through her. The big cock filling her drove her higher and higher until she was wailing at the top of her lungs. She exploded into a state of sheer ecstasy. Her senses curled around her and she floated in a state of euphoria, barely aware of time or space.

"Ash. You okay?"

The words drew her back and she opened her eyes. Dare stared at her in concern.

"You lost consciousness." Adam stood by the side of the bed, holding her hand.

"You made me faint?" She giggled. "Well, we definitely have to do that again."

Dare chuckled and held her close. Adam climbed into bed, too, and held both of them.

"Oh, God, this is so wonderful." She sighed.

She couldn't believe this was what life was going to be like from now on. Two incredibly sexy men to share her bed and her life with. A family that they would create together, on their own terms. She was definitely the luckiest woman in the world.